Royal House of Corinthia

Royally wed...by Christmas!

This Christmas, Princess Arianna and Crown Prince Armando of Corinthia are facing the biggest challenges of their lives.

Pregnant Arianna flees to New York to find some privacy...only to find her very own Prince Charming!

Christmas Baby for the Princess
Available now

Crown Prince Armando needs a royal
so why can't he stop thinking about his
Rosa Lamberti?

Winter Wedding for the Pr
Available December 2

You won't want to miss this
emotional new duet from B
brimming with Christ

Dec 16

Dear Reader,

Welcome to Corinthia, an idyllic country off the Amalfi Coast known for leather products, beautiful countryside and centuries-old traditions.

Unfortunately, life isn't too idyllic for Princess Arianna, daughter of Corinthia's king. In trying to please her father, she made a very big mistake. One with lasting repercussions! Now she's run away to New York City so she can think through an impossible decision: marry a man she doesn't love or disgrace her family by having an illegitimate child.

Just when things couldn't get worse, she's robbed and left penniless!

Enter restaurant owner Max Brown to save the day. Problem is, in saving Arianna he might very well lose his heart. As for Arianna...falling for Max is a complication she definitely doesn't need. Too bad his matinee-idol looks and kind heart make him irresistible.

I know I say this for every book, but I really did have a blast writing this story. Not only did I get to make up my own country, but I also got to incorporate my love of old movies and write a holiday romance. Who can resist falling in love while snow is falling, holiday decorations are twinkling away and a black-and-white film is playing low on the television?

This is the first book in a series featuring the royal family of Corinthia. Next month, you'll meet Arianna's brother, Armando. In the meantime, if you enjoyed Arianna and Max's romance, please let me know at Barbara@BarbaraWallace.com. I hope you have a wonderful holiday season.

Barbara

Christmas Baby for the Princess

Barbara Wallace

—

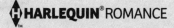

HARLEQUIN®ROMANCE

Recycling programs
for this product may
not exist in your area.

ISBN-13: 978-0-373-74408-4

Christmas Baby for the Princess

First North American Publication 2016

Copyright © 2016 by Barbara Wallace

This edition published by arrangement with Harlequin Books S.A.

For questions and comments about the quality of this book, please contact us at CustomerService@Harlequin.com.

H HARLEQUIN®

www.Harlequin.com

Printed in U.S.A.

Barbara Wallace can't remember when she wasn't dreaming up love stories in her head, so writing romances for Harlequin Romance is a dream come true. Happily married to her own Prince Charming, she lives in New England with a house full of empty-nest animals. Occasionally her son comes home, as well.

To stay up-to-date on Barbara's news and releases, sign up for her newsletter at barbarawallace.com.

Books by Barbara Wallace

Harlequin Romance

The Vineyards of Calanetti

Saved by the CEO

In Love with the Boss

A Millionaire for Cinderella
Beauty & Her Billionaire Boss

The Billionaire's Fair Lady
The Courage to Say Yes
The Man Behind the Mask
Swept Away by the Tycoon
The Unexpected Honeymoon

Visit the Author Profile page
at Harlequin.com for more titles.

To Susan, Selena and Donna, whose emails
help get me from page one to page 220.
And to Peter, my personal Prince Charming.
Merry Christmas, sweetie.

CHAPTER ONE

HER WALLET WAS MISSING.

Arianna was going to be sick. Stomach churning, she slumped against the brick wall and took a shaky breath. Then she checked her bag a third time.

Lipstick. Hand sanitizer. Passport. No wallet.

How? She distinctly remembered double-checking her bag after paying for breakfast, and her wallet had been there, nestled against the silk lining.

Times Square. There'd been that woman who accosted her and needed help reading the subway map, and another man who jostled her while she was trying to break free. One of them must have reached in while she wasn't paying attention…

Stupid, stupid, stupid. This was what happened when you tried to run away from your problems: you got more. Arianna closed her eyes to keep the tears from burning their way free. A few weeks, a month at most—that was all she'd needed.

For what had to be the one-hundredth time, she cursed her own foolishness. If she had listened to her instincts, she never would have had to run away in the first place. She wouldn't have to decide between a loveless marriage and a royal scandal.

Now, thanks to the pickpocket, she was going to have to make the choice sooner rather than later. Without money, she couldn't stay in America. She had no money for food, not to mention that the owner of that terrible hotel where she was staying expected her to pay her bill at the end of the week or, as he so sweetly said, he would toss her pretty rear end on the street.

Her *child* deserved better.

Amazing how one tiny pink line could change your life. When she first missed her period, she blamed stress. After all she and Manolo had just broken up. Besides, they had only been together—like *that*—two times. Two misguided attempts at deepening feelings that weren't there.

When the second month came and went,

however, she couldn't blame stress anymore. The world stopped turning the moment she saw that extra pink line. She didn't know what do to, so she ran. Disappeared, so she could decide which of her no-win choices was the lesser of two evils.

Just then, a cold November wind blew down the street, the chill swirling around her shins before creeping up her skirt. Nature's way of reminding her how serious her predicament really was. Tucking her collar about her throat, Arianna lifted her chin with royal stoicism. No sense dragging her feet. With luck, a decision about what to do would come to her while she was on a plane back to Corinthia.

A few feet ahead, a deliveryman exited one of the businesses, maneuvering his cart over the threshold with a clank loud enough to be heard over Manhattan traffic. The place was called the Fox Club, according to the letters emblazed on the side of the maroon awning. Goodness only knew what kind of club the place was, but no matter. It was open and, hopefully, had a telephone she could borrow.

Except it wasn't a club. It was a time portal.

How else to describe what lay on the other side of the door?

The room looked like it belonged in an old-fashioned American detective movie, like the ones they sometimes played on television late at night. High-backed booths covered in rich burgundy leather, wood so dark it was almost black. Iridescent glass chandeliers that bathed the room with a smoky white light. The hair on Arianna's arms started to rise. Sleek and sensual, the entire space pulsed with expectancy. A simmering promise of *something* for all who walked in.

To her left, a large bar lined the wall. More dark wood, only this time the dark was accented with brass rails and shelves filled with glassware. A stocky black man, dressed to fit the setting, stood by the register. His pomade-slicked head was bent over a clipboard, on which he was making notes. The man didn't look up when she approached.

Arianna cleared her throat. His attention still on the clipboard, the man reached under the bar and produced a sheet of paper that he thrust toward her. "Fill this out. I'll tell the owner you're here."

"Excuse me?"

"You're here about the job, right?"

He hooked a thumb at a sign that had been discreetly tucked in the corner of one of the windows. Through the glass, she could make out the backward outline that read Help Wanted.

"I…"

Arianna paused. It was a silly idea. Her, working in a restaurant. She'd never worked a day in her life. Not a proper job anyway.

On the other hand, if she could find a job, she would earn money, and money meant she could postpone going home.

She would have time to think.

Make the right choice.

Ignoring the voice telling her she was making yet another reckless decision, she set her bag on the bar and, before she could change her mind, announced, "Yes. Yes, I would like the job."

"I appreciate the enthusiasm," a voice replied. A low, smooth voice that definitely did not belong to the bartender.

Arianna looked up and caught her breath. If the club looked like something out of a movie, this man was the movie star. He approached her end of the bar with an elegance that was almost surreal in its smoothness, his double-breasted suit shifting and swaying in a cadence only a custom-made garment could achieve.

His cheekbones were sharp enough to cut glass while his eyes were the color of Mediterranean slate. Only a slightly crooked nose prevented his face from complete perfection. Interestingly, the flaw fit him perfectly. As did his surroundings.

"Max Brown," he said.

Arianna started to nod, the way she always did when someone presented themself, then remembered where she was and quickly stuck out her hand. "Arianna."

"Nice to meet you, Arianna." His grip was solid and sure. "Is there a last name?"

"Santoro." Arianna cringed as her real name popped out.

Fortunately, he showed no signs of recognition. "Pleasure to meet you, Arianna Santoro. You're interested in the waitressing job, are you?"

"Yes, I am."

"Glad to hear it. Have you filled out an application?"

"Not yet," the bartender said.

"I only just walked in," Arianna explained.

His smile was as charming as could be. "That's all right. Why don't we have a seat, and we can fill in the spaces as we go along." He motioned toward one of the booths lining the wall. "We don't need much. Just the usual stuff. Name, address, social security number. Oh, and your firstborn child, of course."

Arianna's stomach lurched.

"Relax, I was only kidding about the first-born part," he said, touching her elbow. "Are you all right?"

"I'm f-fine." She supposed it was nerves making her feel queasy. What was she going to say when he asked for details about her identity? Squeezing the bar rail, she focused on breathing through her nose, hoping the lump would work its way back down. Having something in her stomach might help, too; it was past lunchtime after all. "Could I get some chamomile tea and dry toast?" she asked the bartender.

"You're ordering food on a job interview?" The man shook his head.

Max continued to keep his hand on her elbow. "Might not be a bad idea, Darius," he said. "I wouldn't mind a fresh cup of coffee."

"You want me to go grind the beans for you, too?"

"And grow the chamomile."

The bartender muttered something about his job description, but obliged nonetheless. As soon as he disappeared behind a swinging door, Arianna felt the grip on her elbow tighten.

"Why don't we take a seat," Max said as he gently pulled her away from the bar rail, "and you can tell me about yourself. Starting with why you want to work for the Fox Club."

If only he knew... "Why does anyone want a job?" she asked as she felt herself being propelled to the booths on the other side of the room.

"Generally, because they need money. Is that why you're looking for work? Because you need money?"

"Of course. Why else?"

He looked her up and down. "No reason."

No sooner had she settled onto the leather bench then Darius returned with a serving tray. "The *toast* will be ready in a minute," he said, his face a scowl as he set a small ceramic teapot in front of her. "You need anything else?"

The question was directed to Max, who immediately smiled. Apparently, he found the bartender's abruptness amusing. "I'm good. You want to sit in on this?"

"No, hiring people is your thing. I'm perfectly happy with my supply order, thank you very much. Liquor bottles don't make special requests." Shooting a scowl in Arianna's direction, he turned and headed back to the bar.

"Don't mind him," Max said, shrugging off his jacket. The cloth of his white shirt strained against his biceps as he rolled up the sleeves. "He isn't nearly as put upon as he likes people to think."

"If you say so." She tried to glance over her shoulder, but the bench was too high to see over.

"Trust me, underneath that brusque exterior beats a very soft heart. Ah, this smells good." Coffee cup raised to his lips, he closed his eyes and inhaled. "We import the beans directly from South America. Our own custom blend."

"Really." She hoped she sounded enthusiastic. Usually, she liked coffee, but lately the aroma made her queasy.

"A bad cup can ruin the whole dining experience. Last thing we want are customers leaving with literally a bad taste in their mouth. Not if we want them to come back."

"No, I suppose you don't." She thought about the five-star meals she'd enjoyed over her lifetime. The coffee, like every aspect of the meal, was always impeccable. It never dawned on her to expect otherwise. "You've clearly paid a lot of attention to details."

"I should hope so. Details are what make or break a restaurant."

Then she suspected the Fox Club was "made" because Max Brown seemed to have thought of everything. Like their booth, for example. Not only did the high seat backs ensure privacy, but they'd been designed for two, essentially making them intimate little nooks.

The atmosphere seemed even closer with someone as exceedingly…solid as Max Brown. Suddenly warm, Arianna slipped off her coat. Underneath her turtleneck sweater, her skin tingled as heat spread across it.

Oblivious to her discomfort, her companion had put down his drink and was chivalrously pouring tea into her mug. "So, getting back to my original question, what makes

you think you should work at the Fox Club?
I mean, besides the fact you need a job."

"I, um…" She reached for a napkin and
dabbed at the dampness forming on her upper
lip. Where on earth was her toast? The stron-
gest of odors was emanating from her cup, a
combination of grass and another plant she
couldn't place. Had chamomile tea always
smelled this noxious? Her stomach lurched
again.

Swallowing back the acid, she started over.
"I don't…I mean, there isn't one specific reason. I…"

"You're new to the city, aren't you?"

"Yes," she breathed, grateful to have an
excuse. "Very. I arrived a few…" She caught
the word *days* before it could slip out. "Weeks
ago. How did you know?"

"Because anyone who's lived in New York
for any length of time knows the Fox Club. At
least if they're in the restaurant business they
do." He paused for another sip of coffee. "So,
you're new to the city, and you need a job."

"Yes."

"Where are you staying?"

"The Dunphy Hotel." Actually, dirty and
dated, the Dunphy barely qualified as hab-

itable, let alone a hotel. It was also the last place anyone would think to look for a princess, which was why she had picked it.

"Interesting selection," Max remarked.

"I'm on a budget."

"I see." Something in his tone made her stomach roll again. This time, a layer of anxiety accompanied the nausea. It wasn't possible that he recognized her, was it? Her fingers absently combed the ends of her hair. She'd been monitoring the headlines since she arrived, and thus far, there had been no mention of her or her running away. Then again, Father would no doubt take great pains to keep her running away private. Even if news had made the press, she'd done her best to alter her appearance. Following advice she gleaned from American crime shows, she cut several inches off her hair and dyed the natural blond color a deep black. Since the Corinthian royal family didn't garner that much attention—the paparazzi preferring their British counterparts—she figured even the most ardent of royalty junkies would be hard-pressed to recognize her.

The gray eyes assessing her from across the table, however, made her wonder. The open scrutiny would make her nervous, whether she was hiding or not. He seemed to be examining every inch of her.

She forced herself to meet his gaze, while pressing a hand to her abdomen. The churning was getting worse. She could feel the acid creeping up her esophagus again.

"Experience…?"

He was talking to her. "Experience in what?" she asked, pressing her lips into a tight smile.

"Waiting tables. Now that the holiday season is getting underway, we're going to be busier than usual. A lot of groups book tables this time of year so we need someone who is used to juggling multiple large parties. Have you done large parties before?"

Swallowing back the queasiness, Arianna nodded. "Several." It wasn't a complete lie. She'd been standing in as her father's hostess since her mother died a decade ago and had assisted in planning more than her fair share of state dinners. Surely, memorizing dinner orders and bringing them to the table couldn't be more difficult than memorizing dignitaries' dossiers and defusing potential international incidents.

"Great. Where?"

"Where?"

"Where did you wait tables?"

"Oh, right. Italy," she replied, falling back on the cover story she'd rehearsed in case someone asked about her accent. Out of all of Corinthia's continental neighbors, the Mediterranean country was the closest in terms of language and culture.

"Any particular location or did you serve the entire country?" While his coffee cup masked much of his mouth, she could still see the hint of a smile.

Naturally he expected more specific details. To buy a few seconds to think, she took a drink, only to gag as soon as the liquid passed her lips. The stuff tasted as botanical as it smelled. Worse, actually. She shoved the cup to the middle of the table.

"Miss Santoro?" Max asked.

"I—"

No good. Her tea, her breakfast and everything else in her stomach jumped to the back of her throat. Clamping a hand to her mouth, she sprinted from the table.

"Second door on your left," Max called out as she rushed away. Not that it mattered all that much with the restaurant empty. So long as she made it to one of the restrooms, they'd be fine.

"What the…?" Darius had just come around the bar carrying a plate of toast. "Usually it takes two or three dates before the woman runs away from you. What happened?"

"Very funny," Max replied. From behind him he heard the soft thud of a restroom door closing. She had made it somewhere at least. "Do me a favor and get a glass of ice water. She's probably going to need a cold drink when she comes out." Poor woman was as green as her tea.

Definitely not your typical job interview. Or applicant, for that matter. Not too many out-of-work waitresses that he knew walked around wearing cashmere. He might not know women's fashion labels by name, but he recognized expensive when he saw it. Besides, she moved like money. That posture screamed "private school."

A cashmere coat, and she was staying at a rat hole like the Dunphy? New to the country or not, the two did not go together. Women as beautiful as her stayed in five-star suites and not alone. They didn't apply for temporary waitress positions.

"You notice the haircut?" Darius asked, returning with the water.

Yeah, Max had noticed. Right after he noticed the coat. A total home job, and not a very good one at that. "She's trying to hide from someone."

"If she's thinking that hair will help her blend in, she's crazy."

It wasn't just her haircut that attracted attention. It was the whole package. "If she wore it up, it'd look okay." Even if it didn't, most people would be too distracted by the rest of her to notice.

"Don't tell me you're considering her."

"Something tells me she's in a tough spot."

"Great. Another one of your lost puppies." If his friend rolled his eyes any further, they would see the inside of his head. "Didn't you learn anything from what happened with Shirley? You can't save the whole world, you know."

"I never said I wanted to save the whole world." The few desperate souls who crossed his path, is all. And just because some, like his former piano player, chose not to be saved, was no reason to stop. It was definitely not a reason in this case.

He lowered his voice in case Arianna happened to come back. "She's staying at the Dunphy."

Darius whistled.

"Exactly." If that wasn't enough of a red flag, there was desperation in her eyes. An anxious shadow that said things weren't as she pretended. Max knew that shadow well. He had seen it in his mother's eyes all her life. Okay, so maybe Arianna wasn't running away from an abusive bastard like his father. But she was running away from something. And there was no way in hell he was turning a desperate woman out in the street. His mother's eyes haunted him enough; he didn't have to add a second pair.

"Besides," he said, shaking off the ghosts, "you've got to admit, she would look amazing in the uniform."

"Maybe, but can she wait tables? All you did this morning was jaw my ear off about how hard it is to find decent help. Do you really want to take the risk? Christmastime is crazy."

"I thought it was the time for goodwill toward men."

"Very funny." A soft cough cut off whatever else Darius was going to say. Arianna had returned to the table. Despite shaking and being white as a sheet, she still managed to look gorgeous and self-possessed. Max felt the stirring of attraction deep in his belly.

"Everything all right?" he asked.

Her nod was as wobbly as her legs. "Fine. That is, I was feeling light-headed, but I'm much better now."

She was a horrible liar. *Better* would mean color in her cheeks.

"Thank you," she said, noticing the water.

"No problem. Figured you wouldn't be looking for the tea." His coffee had long since grown cold, but he drank it anyway. Wasn't the first time—wouldn't be the last. "So," he said, from over the rim, "you were telling me about where you used to work."

Her eyes immediately dropped to her glass. "Right. Where I worked. The thing is…"

"It was a long time ago?" he suggested.

"Exactly." She grabbed the excuse like a lifeline, gratitude in her voice. "I'm not sure they would remember me."

Max sat back and took a good look at her, trying to think like the businessman he was.

Ten to one, the only experience she had waitressing involved leaving a tip. Darius was right: he had no business offering her a job.

But then he saw how hard she was struggling to keep her composure and his conscience beat down his common sense.

"That's all right," he said, "I'll take your word for it. Do you think you will feel well enough to start tomorrow night?"

Her eyes widened. "I have the job?"

In a flash, Max understood how every private eye in every mystery movie fell prey to the femme fatale. The way her face lit up was absolutely criminal. He smoothed his tie and did his best to hide his reaction. "You did say you wanted it, didn't you?"

"I did. I mean, I do." She leaned forward, the subtle scent of high-end perfume accompanying her. "Thank you so much," she said, clasping his hands. "You have no idea how much this means to me."

Definitely criminal. Reluctantly, he disentangled himself from her grasp and stood up. "Darius will go over everything you need to know, including where to get your uniform. Welcome to the Fox Club family, Miss Santoro."

Out of the corner of his eye, he could see Darius shaking his head. Honestly, sometimes his friend was too much the glass-half-empty kind of guy. They were helping a gorgeous woman out of a tight spot, is all. What was the worst that could happen?

CHAPTER TWO

SHE WAS THE worst waitress he'd ever seen. Quite possibly, the worst waitress on the planet.

"I tried to tell you," Darius said, sliding Max a cup of coffee. "But you and your white-knight complex wouldn't listen."

Biting back the retort he wanted to give, Max forced his features to remain expressionless. "She's a bit rusty, I'll give you that."

"Rusty? The past two nights she's dropped three trays. Not to mention all the orders she's messed up. Lorenzo and his staff are annoyed—they're threatening to refuse any order she puts in."

"Yeah, well, Lorenzo better think twice about that, considering I'm about to drop a small fortune upgrading the kitchen."

"It's not just Lorenzo. Darlene and the other waitresses are annoyed, too. Apparently she keeps disappearing into the employees' lounge during her shift."

So Max had noticed. In fact, he'd been paying quite a lot of attention to his newest employee the past two days. Enough to realize it wasn't only his desire to help that had made him hire her. She looked breathtaking in the waitress costume. He'd personally ordered the dress after seeing a photograph of Grace Kelly wearing something similar, the idea being that his waitresses would be smoldering but classy. On Arianna, the concept took on a whole new meaning. Every man in the room had to be cursing how the neckline didn't dip low enough to reveal anything more than bare shoulders and a hint of cleavage. Max certainly was.

She'd fixed her hair, too. Pulled it into some fancy twist that showed off a long, graceful neck. Max had dated his share of women—beautiful women—but none as enticing as his new waitress. As a rule, he didn't get involved with the help—made for an awkward work environment when he moved on—but with Arianna, he was seriously tempted.

"Darlene asked her if she was sick, and she insisted she wasn't," Darius said. "You don't suppose she's using, do you?"

"Nah." Enough addicts and alcoholics had crossed his path over the years for him to know the signs. "Nervous stomach, more likely." He'd caught her stealing crackers from the salad bar. "All the same, tell the other waitresses to let me know if they see anything odd."

"That mean you're going to let her keep waiting tables?"

"How else is she going to get up-to-speed? Another day or two and she'll be fine."

There was a loud crash.

"Another day or two, huh?" Darius said. "You sure?"

Across the room, their newest employee had just spilled a salad on... Oh, Lord—was that the deputy mayor?

Max ran a hand over his face. "Send a couple bottles of Amatucci reserve to the table, and tell him the entire night is on the house." He watched as the mayor's right-hand man slapped away Arianna's hand before plucking a piece of arugula from the lapel of his gray flannel suit. Hopefully the drink and a few profuse apologies would be enough to soothe the man's ego.

"And your new puppy? What about her?"

"Move her to somewhere where she won't cause damage for the rest of the night," he said.

"You mean you're not going to let her go?"

He'd certainly fired employees for less. Only he couldn't shake the memory of her anxious expression, or that she was in a roach hotel to beat all roach hotels. Attraction to her aside, there remained the fact she was a woman clearly looking for an escape. What kind of man would he be if he cut her loose?

"Tomorrow we'll try her at the hostess station." Now that he thought about it, he should have assigned her that position to begin with. Who wouldn't want to follow her to their table?

"You're the boss," Darius said, with a look that said he disagreed. "I just hope you know what you're doing."

So did he, thought Max. So did he.

"Arianna, may I speak to you for a moment?"

The fussy, nasal voice of the maître d' had the uncanny ability to cut through the restaurant din like an upper-crust trumpet. By itself the tone was enough to make Arianna's insides cringe. When coupled with the distinct sound of disapproval, it made her feel sick to her stomach. Or *sicker*, as the case may be. What had she done this time?

Javier stood at his seating station, impatiently tapping his pen against the wood. His rigid posture reminded her of the music instructor her father had hired when she was twelve. A dictatorial virtuoso who she'd been certain had moonlighted as a prison guard. Come to think of it, she wouldn't be surprised if Javier moonlighted at the same place.

Smoothing the front of her waitress dress, which was doubling as a hostess outfit for the evening, she excused herself from the diners with whom she'd been talking and headed toward him. He immediately tilted his gel-slicked head toward a corner away from the crowd. "I thought I asked you to seat the last party in section four," he said, once they were out of earshot.

"I did." At least she thought she had.

"No, you seated them in section three."

Section three, section four...what difference did it make? Four people needed a table, so she gave them a table with four chairs.

Apparently, from the maître d's dramatic sigh, it mattered a great deal. "Did I not tell you that restaurant seating is like a mathematical equation? You make a mistake on one side of the dining room, then the entire scheme is thrown off-balance. Now I'm going to have to redo the entire seating chart. Again."

Arianna lifted her chin. Perhaps, she wanted to say, if she'd been allowed more than five minutes to study the floor plan before the restaurant opened... Traditionally, memorizing information on quick order wasn't a problem, but lately it seemed her brain was constantly foggy and sluggish. It did not help that the majority of her energy these days seemed to center on trying not to run to the ladies' room.

Apparently, Javier wasn't done lecturing her. "And did you tell a couple they couldn't sit in one of the back booths?"

"They were walk-ins. You told me the booths were reserved."

"I also told you customer service is our number-one priority. As the first face they see when they come into the Fox Club, you are in a sense Mr. Brown's ambassador, and as such, you never tell a customer you cannot accommodate their request."

"But I thought I wasn't supposed to disrupt the seating chart."

Javier glared at her. "From now on, come and get me if there's a special request. I don't want you making decisions on your own." He reached for the reservation book while muttering under his breath. Arianna caught the words *empty-headed* and *useless*.

They were enough to make her see red. Raising herself to her fullest height, she stared down her nose at the maître d'. "Listen here, you…"

"Excuse me." A tall, elderly woman approached them, preventing Arianna from finishing. The newcomer wore a pale green gown that, while dated, Arianna immediately recognized from the stitching as a designer original. She was carrying a leather tote bag and a large brown canister.

"Javier," she said, in an upper-crust voice to rival the maître d's. Another time, Arianna would find it amusing that she, the actual royal, had the least affected voice. "It's five past seven. Mr. Riderman and I distinctly requested a seven o'clock reservation. I mentioned it to this young woman, but she told me I had to wait."

"The rest of her party hasn't arrived yet," Arianna told Javier, figuring that he would appreciate the defense, since he set the rule.

He didn't, though. He snapped to even greater attention. "My apologies, Mrs. Riderman. She is a new employee. Had I seen you walk in I would have attended to you personally. May I send you and Mr. Riderman a cocktail with our compliments?"

The elderly woman's hand fluttered at the offer, her gigantic cocktail ring spinning on her thin finger as she did. "Mr. Riderman isn't drinking this evening. I, however, will have an extra dry martini."

"Very good." Arianna had to force herself not to roll her eyes at the bow Javier offered the woman. The palace guards weren't that effusive. "Now if you follow me, your regular table is ready."

There was another exception to his rules? If he was going to allow exceptions, then there should be a list for employees.

Javier glared at her when he returned. "You are very lucky, Mrs. Riderman is a forgiving person," he said.

Oh, no, she refused to let some uptight little man lecture her on this. "You specifically instructed that no party was to be seated unless everyone was present."

"The entire party *was* present."

"No, Mr. Riderman…" She stopped, suddenly remembering the bronze vase. "You mean she is eating with her dead husband's…?"

"Will you keep your voice down?" he said, almost hissing. "Mrs. Riderman is one of our oldest and best customers. She's also an influential voice in the New York arts society."

Who eats with her husband's ashes? "Does Mr. Brown know about this?"

"Of course he knows."

"Oh." And he wasn't disturbed? "I'm sorry. I'll make sure that doesn't happen again." The next time a party arrived carrying a jar of remains, she'd make sure to seat them promptly.

"It most certainly will not," Javier replied. "You've done quite enough damage for the evening."

Arianna stiffened as he touched her elbow. She still wasn't used to being touched so casually. In Corinthia, only her family and closest confidants took such liberties.

And Manolo, she added ruefully. He had taken a lot of liberties. But then, she'd been foolish enough to think the words coming out of his mouth were sincere.

"Are you sending me home?"

Javier shook his head. "Only Max can do that." Arianna was certain she heard a silent "unfortunately" prefacing the sentence. "For now, I just want you out of the way."

"Doing what?" As if she couldn't guess.

Folding tableware. Tucked away at the corner of the bar, with a stack of linen napkins and a silverware tray in front of her, she was quickly becoming an expert at the task.

Take a napkin off the pile, fold the cloth carefully into a triangle and stack a knife and two forks by the fold. Then tuck the corners to keep the silverware in place before rolling them into a cylinder. Within five minutes she'd built a small pyramid. At this rate, the restaurant would have table settings to last until New Year's.

She should have called home by now. If she was back home, she'd be curled up in her big comfortable bed right now waiting for a servant to bring her a cup of lavender mint tea.

Instead, her feet hurt, her back hurt and her

stomach wouldn't stop lurching from the constant food smells passing by her nose. All she wanted to do was close her eyes and sleep for the next twenty-four hours straight.

Worse, after three days, she was no closer to deciding what she should do.

As if on cue, a wave of nausea hit her, forcing her to press a fist to her lips. If she didn't know better, she'd say the child inside her was voicing its opinion. Too bad she did not know what side the bambino was on. Then again, how could an embryo know what to do when she herself didn't?

If only she had not seen Manolo's true colors. Then perhaps the idea of spending a lifetime with him would not seem so…daunting. Her father, of course, was thoroughly impressed by the man and had been thrilled when she and the industrialist began dating. A wedding and grandchild would send him over the moon.

But wasn't wanting to please Father what had gotten her into this dilemma? Knowing how happy the relationship made her father, she'd ignored the questions whispering in her ear. If Manolo's kisses failed to make her head spin, or if there were times when she thought he loved being with the king more than with her, it was her imagination. After all, no relationship was perfect one hundred percent of the time. Perhaps if they were intimate her doubts would disappear...

Finding another woman's underwear in his apartment had shown her how wrong that idea was. Unfortunately, the shutters were pulled from her eyes a little too late.

"You're doing that wrong," a voice said from behind her.

Max. A quiver struck low in her stomach. The bambino seemed to have an opinion about him as well. Since that first day, her stomach insisted on wobbling every time she and the owner crossed paths.

He reached over her shoulder to take the setting from her hand. "The ends have to be tucked tightly or else the silverware will slide out. See?"

Arianna could feel his breath on the back of her bare neck. In Corinthia, it was considered disrespectful to stand so close to a member of the royal family. A deferential distance had to be maintained at all times. Max's arms were nearly wrapped around her. She could feel the edge of his jacket brushing her spine

as he leaned forward, the feathery touch causing goose bumps.

"Now you try."

She tried to repeat the steps she'd done doz-
ens of times throughout the night, but her
fingers had grown clumsy. Instead of stack-
ing the silverware, she fumbled and knocked
them over. "It would be easier if you weren't
breathing down my neck," she told him.

"Sorry." The space behind her cooled as he
took a spot at the bar next to her chair. Better,
but not by much. Arianna could still feel his
slate-colored eyes watching her every move.
Taking a deep breath, she rolled the napkin
into the tightest cylinder humanly possible.

"Good," Max said. "Although next time,
you might want to include a spoon."

Her shoulders sagged. Out of the corner of
her eye, she saw Darius slide a drink across
the bar. Max wrapped his hand around it
without looking, and settled back against the
bar rail to survey the restaurant. Unable to
help herself, Arianna stole a look.

The man had the most effortless grace
about him. You could see it in the way the
glass dangled from his long fingertips and in
the way he moved. Yet for all his smoothness,

he wasn't overly soft. Just like how the scar on the bridge of his nose kept his face from movie-star perfection, there was strength beneath the elegance. A toughness that said he wasn't a man to be trifled with. In a way he reminded her of the ancestral portraits lining the halls of Corinthia Castle, with their impenetrable gazes that followed her every step.

They always left her feeling very exposed, those paintings. Max's stare did as well.

"I hear you're having trouble catching on to hostessing," he said, his gaze thankfully still on the dining room.

Trouble catching on had to be an American euphemism for making a lot of mistakes. "It was not all my fault," she said, defensiveness kicking in. "No one told me the woman was deluded."

"I beg your pardon?"

"The woman in the green dress. How was I to know she wanted a seat for her husband's remains?"

"Ah, Mrs. Riderman." Understanding crested over his features. "You're right, Javier should have warned you. She and her 'husband' come in every Friday."

"Every week?" With her dead husband?

"Does that not violate some kind of health code?"

"Probably," he said with a shrug, "but seeing how she owns most of the buildings on this street, we're willing to risk the infraction."

"Oh." Whatever vindication she felt faded away. "I did not realize she was so important."

"All our customers are important," Max corrected. "Without them, we wouldn't exist." He took a sip of his drink. "Did he tell you that every time you move a party or seat them at the wrong table, that he needs to redo the seating chart?"

More times than she could count. "Yes," she said.

"Did he also tell you that having to start over causes even longer delays?"

"No, that he did not mention."

Arianna fiddled with the napkin roll she'd just completed, twirling the black cloth back and forth between her fingers. Whereas being upbraided by the likes of Javier set her teeth on edge, Max's criticisms made her feel foolish and inept. She couldn't imagine him ever making as many mistakes as she had these past few days.

"I had some trouble memorizing the seating chart," she said meekly. "My brain, it…"

She shook her head. Max didn't need to hear how her brain had become fuzzy and sluggish, or how it took all her energy to keep her ever-present morning sickness at bay.

"I'm sorry," she said instead. "I'll pay closer attention in the future."

"Afraid it's too late for that. Javier's refusing to let you back up front."

"He is?" That was not fair. She did not make that many mistakes. "What am I supposed to do then?" Surely they had enough tableware.

Max didn't reply, beyond staring into his drink. "I don't know," he said after a moment. "You can't hostess for Javier anymore. And I can't put you back out there as a waitress. Not after what happened with Deputy Mayor Esperanza. The man you dumped a salad on last night," he added when she gave him a blank look.

That man was the deputy mayor? While Corinthia didn't have the position, she knew enough about the title to assume that in a city the size of New York, the title was an important one. "No wonder he asked if I knew who he was."

She must have said something amusing because the hint of a smile played on Max's
mouth. "Yes, well, Deputy Mayor Esperanza
is a legend in his own mind, that is for sure."

"Was he very angry?" If the way the man
turned a deep shade of crimson was any indication, he had been. She'd done her best to
apologize, but the horrid little man simply
slapped her words aside and told her to leave
him alone.

"Nothing a couple bottles of super Tuscan
didn't cure," Max replied.

"Good." She would have felt terrible if her
mistake caused real damage to Max's restaurant. "I'm glad."

"Me, too. Although between you and me,
the guy could use an arugula shower now and
then. To keep him humble."

Setting his drink on the counter, he shifted
his posture, leaning his weight on the elbow
closest to the bar so he once again faced her.
The smile he'd been fighting had found its
way to his eyes, the shine bringing out flecks
of blue in them Arianna hadn't noticed before. Her lips curled upward in response and
for a moment, they silently shared the idea.

"So," Max said, reaching for his drink

again. "You've never waited tables before, have you?"

"Of course I ha— How did you know?"

He arched his brow. "Did you seriously think I wouldn't notice your lack of experience?"

"No." Certainly not with the way he was watching her. Still... Her cheeks growing hot, she looked down at her feet. "I had hoped I would catch on quickly."

"How's that plan working out?"

"Not so well."

"You think?"

She'd prefer anger to sarcasm. "If you knew, why did you hire me?"

"Because I'm a sucker for a sob story, that's why," he replied.

Sob story? "I did not tell—"

"You didn't have to," he said, frowning into the last of his drink. "I guess I'd hoped you'd catch on quickly, too."

But she hadn't, and she felt like a fool for even trying. "I didn't realize it would be so difficult." All those people speaking so rapidly, barking orders at her. "Everything moves so much faster than I expected."

"Problem is, this is our busiest season. I

need a waitress who can be up-to-speed immediately. I don't have the time to train someone."

"I understand," Arianna replied, though that didn't take away the sting. Before, she'd been merely foolish. Now she was foolish and useless, too.

Seemed like all she'd done the past few weeks was let people down. Her lower lip started to quiver. How on earth was she going to be able to do what was right for a baby? She hadn't so far.

"I'll go get my coat."

Sliding off the stool to her feet, she barely got a step before Max's hand caught her arm. "Hold on," he said. "You don't have to go so fast."

What was the point in staying? So she could fold more napkins?

"We're on the last round of seating. Why don't you grab a good hot meal, and wait until closing. I'll take you home, and we can talk about what you're going to do. Okay?"

How could she say no when his eyes were filled with such concern? Seeing their warmth helped to soften her disappointment. If she had one good memory about her brief stay in New York, Max Brown looking at her right now, with soft, sexy, sympathetic eyes, would be it.

Plus, she would be foolish to turn down a five-star meal. Her stomach, with its usual unpredictability, leaped for joy when he made the offer. "All right," she said. "I'll wait."

"Good." He looked pleased. Maybe it was wishful thinking, but she swore he had looked as disappointed about her imminent departure as she felt. "I'll send Darlene over with a menu.

"And hey, chin up…" His fingers caught her jaw, tilting her face toward his. "Everything will work out. You'll see."

"Sure," she whispered after he left. "We'll see."

Leaving Arianna at the bar, Max retreated to the sanctuary of his office. He had the sudden need to bury himself in paperwork and clear away thoughts of pale skin and black sateen dresses.

What was he going to do? His office chair squeaked as he collapsed into it. There was no way he could keep Arianna on staff; the woman was a disaster. Javier spent ten minutes ranting about her inabilities and swearing on his mother's life that he would not work with "that woman" again. Over-the-top? Sure, but the man was also one of the finest maître d's in the city. Max couldn't risk ticking him off. Especially since he'd had a similar "discussion" with his chef the night before.

So what did he do? He choked. He'd walked out there to fire her, but right when he was about to say the words, they died on his tongue. Killed by a pair of soulful blue eyes.

His mother's eyes had been brown. Brown and surrounded by mottled purple smudges she would try to cover with makeup. It never worked. Max always knew. No matter how much she applied, makeup couldn't cover split lips.

Not for the first time, he wondered if Arianna was running away from the same nightmare as his mother. His gut said no. Well, his gut and the fact that her alabaster skin would bruise too easily for her to hide it.

Or maybe he was rationalizing to soothe his conscience.

His conscience was still nagging him a few hours later when Darius knocked on his office door. "Just wanted to let you know the last party is getting ready to leave," he said.

"Thanks. I'll be out to close out the till in a bit."

"Okay." Except instead of leaving, his friend wavered in the doorway. "Is it true?" he asked. "Did you really let your new puppy go?"

"Stop calling her that," Max said, bristling. Arianna wasn't some stray off the streets. "And who told you I let her go?"

"The pup—lady—herself. When Darlene brought over a steak, she told me it was her last meal at the Fox Club."

"Oh." Apparently, he'd made his point after all. Now his conscience really stung. "I suppose it is."

"It's for the best, you know."

"I know." Didn't mean he had to be happy about it, though.

Stepping all the way inside the office, the bartender pushed aside the brass lamp and took its place on the edge of Max's desk. "Look, man, no one appreciates what you were trying to do more than me, but things don't always work out, you know? If you still want to help her, write the chick a check. Unless..."

His voice drifting off, Darius's attention shifted to the desk's surface and an invisible spot that he suddenly needed to scratch at with his fingernail.

Max narrowed his eyes. "Unless what?"

"Unless, it ain't just about helping a girl out. You said yourself she was hot."

"I didn't say she was hot, I said she'd look good in the uniform…and I was right." Over on the side of the desk, Darius let out a snort. One that said Max was splitting hairs, and they both knew it.

Truth? Yeah, he was attracted to the woman. She was different from other women who had crossed his path, and not because her appearance screamed money—although that did make her stand out. It was her personality that truly set her apart. She had the oddest combination of haughtiness and innocence about her. One moment she was icy and entitled, the next she looked vulnerable and scared. Most women, he could read from the get-go. They were either women from his old life, looking to rise up from their lousy circumstances, or they were women from his current world looking to hook a successful businessman. In either case, their faces were open books.

Not Arianna's, though. As much as he could read her, there was a layer he couldn't get to. It intrigued him.

Excited him, too. The way she wore that uniform, like it was a real Dior. He'd have to be a dead man not to appreciate that fact, and even death wasn't a guarantee that he wouldn't, seeing as how every swish of her skirt and sway of her hips sent awareness shooting below his belt.

A smile played on his lips. "Oh, brother," Darius said. "Just admit you want her already, will you?"

Max refused to respond. Spinning in his chair, he turned and looked out his office window. The view wasn't much, an alley and the emergency exit for the building on the next lot, but he'd certainly had worse. Behind him, the dining room was quiet except for the sounds of chairs being put on the tables. In between scrapes and rattles, he heard the soft notes of a piano over the din. Some song he'd never heard before. Reminded him of a Christmas carol, but not quite.

"When did you switch on the radio?" he asked. Normally, he wasn't big on plain piano music, but this was nice.

"I didn't," Darius replied. "That's the piano on stage."

"Are you sure?"

"Positive. Unless the speaker over your door is blown."

Max frowned. "Shirley?" Last he heard, his former piano player was behind bars. "You think she got out?"

"Doubt it. Besides, she was never that good."

Rising, Max made his way to the office door, with Darius not far behind. Together the two of them stepped into the main dining room. "Well, what do you know...?" Max said, giving a low whistle.

Arianna sat the piano, head bent over the keyboard, playing with the agility of a trained expert.

CHAPTER THREE

ONCE SHE FINISHED her dinner, Arianna didn't know what to do with herself. Most of the patrons were gone, and the staff was busy getting ready to close. From the looks they gave her, it was clear they did not want her assistance.

She couldn't sit there and do nothing. Her nerves wouldn't let her. In a little while Max would emerge from his office to walk her home, ending her career at the Fox Club. She would be back to where she started three days ago: looking for a way to postpone her return home. Only this time, she doubted there would be another handsome white knight waiting to ride to the rescue.

Looking around, her attention stopped at the piano on the stage. She'd noticed it her first day here, but had yet to take a close look. Her spirits picked up a little. Surely no one would mind if she looked now. Reclaiming her heels, having kicked them off while eating, she slipped them on and headed over.

For as long as she could remember, the piano had been a close friend. When she was a little girl, she would sit on the bench next to her mother and accompany her by plunking out random notes. Later, the discipline of practice helped her survive the pain of losing her mama. And again when she mourned her sister-in-law's death.

Of course her instructors would say those were the only times she appreciated discipline since she spent most of her childhood ditching formal practice in favor of playing lighter, more enjoyable pieces.

She hadn't played much when she was dating Manolo; he'd been more interested in being seen than in listening to her play. The club's baby grand might not have as sophisticated a soundboard as the palace piano, but it was in excellent condition, and more importantly, she thought as she smiled and pressed middle C, it was in tune. Taking a seat on its bench felt a little bit like greeting a long lost friend.

Stretching her fingers, she played a scale,

followed by an arpeggio. Because she was rusty, her fingers fumbled, and for a moment, it was like when she tried rolling tableware. Quickly, though, she loosened up, and the notes began to flow with ease. Confidence restored, she started playing one of the handful of songs she knew from memory: "In the Bleak Midwinter." The quiet, melancholy song seemed fitting, given her circumstances.

When she finished, she realized everyone in the club was watching her. Including Max, who stood near the front of the stage.

"Bravo," he said, clapping. "That was amazing."

Arianna blushed as satisfaction swept her from head to toe. Her entire life, people had showered her with compliments regarding her playing, and she'd basked in them all, but none of the accolades had affected her as much as seeing the admiration on Max's face was. Knowing she had his approval left a thrill that started at the base of her spine and spread outward, to the ends of her fingers.

He hopped onto the stage to join her. "You've been keeping secrets. Why didn't you tell me you could play the piano?"

"I didn't realize it was important," she replied. After all, she'd applied for a job as a waitress. If she had known it was important, she would have touted her skills first thing.

"Play something else," one of the waiters called out.

"Sounds like you've won at least one fan. How about it? You got any other songs tucked in that pretty head of yours?"

"A few." Running through her mental library she decided upon a Corinthian folk song, a simple melody that had been a childhood favorite. She did her best to ignore the fact that Max was watching her. Hard to do with him propped against the curve of the piano, his long fingers curled around the rim.

"Pretty," he said, after she'd been playing a moment. He was smiling, bringing the blue to his eyes again. "How long have you been playing?"

"Since I was old enough to sit at the bench without falling over," she replied, adding a glissando for flourish.

"That old."

"My mother played. When I was little, I would watch her. Playing was a natural progression."

He leaned forward, a curious look on his face. "I don't suppose you sing, too?"

"Perhaps." If only he knew. Both she and her brother had to study voice. One could hardly lead the people in the Corinthian anthem off-key. "Why do you ask?"

"No reason. I was curious, is all. I have to close out the till. Would you mind playing a little longer? I think people are enjoying the concert."

Arianna looked out at the waitstaff, some of whom were nodding their heads in time with the music as they worked. Even Javier looked to be tapping his foot. "But of course," she said. It would be nice to leave them on a positive note after so many mishaps.

She played every song she could remember, an eclectic combination that ranged from Beethoven to Bocelli. Finally, there was but one song left that she could play from memory: "*Tu Scendi dale Stelle*," a popular Italian carol her grandmother used to sing. She hadn't meant to sing, but the words came out automatically.

In a flash, her head filled with memories of home. Of making candied fruit for Babbo Natale and pastries for Christmas Eve and how the whole country seemed to smell of evergreen and wine. So many traditions and she loved them all. She was Corinthian to the core.

Her heart jumped to her throat, choking off the words. She couldn't go on. "I'm sorry," she whispered as she stepped off the stage.

Max came out of his office as she was rushing toward the coatroom. "Is everything all right?"

She couldn't answer; the lump was still stuck in her throat. Brushing past him, she kept going until she was safely shut in with the coats and hangers. There she squeezed her eyes tight.

This was ridiculous. Getting emotional over a Christmas song. So what if the words reminded her of home? It wasn't as if she wouldn't be returning to Corinthia again.

Although if she chose not to marry Manolo, she would lose the country's respect, and that was as bad as never going home at all.

Footsteps sounded behind her. "Arianna? What's wrong?"

"Nothing is wrong," she told him, sniffing. "I felt a little homesick for a moment, that's all."

"Homesick, huh? Maybe this will help."

Out of nowhere, a handkerchief appeared before her. It was such an old-fashioned, chivalrous gesture that she couldn't help smiling as she dabbed at her eyes. The square smelled faintly of aftershave. Woody and masculine. Without thinking about what she was doing, she pressed the cloth to her nose and inhaled the scent. "Are you always this prepared?"

"If you're asking whether or not I'm a Boy Scout, absolutely not. I've just learned to keep a handkerchief on hand in case I run in to emotional women."

"Do you run in to them often?"

"More often than you'd think, unfortunately"

And what would they be crying for? she wondered. Because he had broken their hearts? It certainly wouldn't surprise her if those slate-colored eyes left a whole trail of women in their wake. Manolo had his assortment of conquests, did he not? And he wasn't nearly as handsome. Or, as gallant.

That gallantry was on full display as he took her coat from the hanger and held it for her to put on. "Where is home exactly?" he asked. "I mean, where in Italy? You are Italian, right? Tell me that much is true."

Arianna paused to enjoy the way his hands settled on her shoulders, the touch providing a comfort she hadn't realized she needed. It would be easy enough to say yes and end the speculation. For some reason, though, she couldn't bring herself to lie to him again. "Close."

"Close?"

"I'm from a small island country off the coast. I doubt you've ever heard of it."

"Probably not," he replied, brushing her shoulders again. "I always sucked at world geography. If a place isn't on one of the six continents, forget it."

"Seven," she said, smiling over her shoulder. She liked how he knew not to ask any more questions.

The grin she got in response made her forget all about homesickness. "Antarctica doesn't deserve full billing, if you ask me. Come on. Let me get my coat, and I'll take you home."

"You know, you really don't have to..." She followed him back into the dining room and into the darkly paneled room that passed as his office. "I will be fine on my own."

"Are you still staying at the Dunphy?" She

nodded. "Then, yes, I do need to escort you. Besides, you and I need to talk about your future."

Which future was that, she was tempted to ask. Because she still hadn't figured out an answer. "I did not think I had a future here," she said instead.

"Did I say that?"

"You said you didn't have time to train me."

"As a waitress, I don't," he said, reaching behind the door for his overcoat. "But you clearly don't need training to play piano."

Arianna's pulse quickened. "Are you suggesting I play the piano? Here?"

"No, at Carnegie Hall. Of course I mean here. It's the perfect solution, really. Every good movie nightclub has a chanteuse."

"A what?"

"A sultry lounge singer. My former one, she was unable to fulfill her contract. I planned to hire someone new after the holidays. Now, I don't have to. You're perfect for the job."

No, she wasn't perfect. Playing piano meant being in the spotlight. Far different from waiting tables or passing out menus, jobs where she had limited interaction with people and if someone recognized her, she could easily claim coincidence.

"I can't," she said, shaking her head. "I'm sorry, but I just can't." She looked away rather than meet his eye.

Several beats of quiet followed, where the only sound in the room was that of him shrugging into his coat. Arianna prayed his silence was because he'd decided to accept her answer without asking for a reason.

"I had a feeling that would be your answer," he said after a moment.

"You did?"

"Like I told you before, I'm not an idiot. Anyone with half a brain can tell you don't want to be recognized."

She should have realized her crude efforts at disguise wouldn't make it past a man as sharp as Max. "How did you figure it out?"

"Honey, I knew the minute you walked through the door. The cashmere coat and do-it-yourself haircut were dead giveaways.

"Don't worry," he added, as her hand flew to her neck. "It looks better pulled up. Makes the haircut look less obvious."

"Here I thought I was being clever."

"You didn't do that bad a job."

"I could not have done a very good one either if I didn't fool you."

"Only because I've seen more than most people."

Like what? What made him different than everyone else?

Because he was different, in so many ways.

Once more, his hands found their way to her shoulders. Despondent as she was, warmth still managed to travel down her arms. Like metal to a magnet, she felt herself leaning against him.

"Look," he said, "I don't know what your story is, but if you're in some kind of trouble…"

Arianna sucked in her breath. Max's breath warming her temple made it difficult to think too clearly, but one message managed to make it through the fog, and that was that he didn't recognize her. He only recognized a woman in hiding.

She relaxed farther into him. "Thank you."

"I'm serious, Arianna. If I can help… If someone is trying to hurt you…"

"No." She whipped around so they were eye to eye. "That is not the case at all!"

"Really?" He looked skeptical.

"Yes, I promise. I never meant to make you

think I was in danger." No wonder he had been so patient with her. "You're right, I don't want to be found, but I'm not in trouble. Not *that* kind of trouble," she said with emphasis. "I just needed a few weeks by myself, to sort out a few things."

"And you needed to change your appearance to do this?"

"It's complicated."

"Most things are." There was a pause as he contemplated what to say. "You know, if you need someone to talk to—"

"Thank you, but this is something I need to handle on my own."

"Okay." Finally, he appeared to let the topic drop. For now at least. "How about we get going then?"

Ever since Max had walked out of his office that first day, Arianna had wondered if, when removed from the vintage surroundings, he would still look like a movie star. He did. The atmosphere followed him. Standing on the sidewalk, she shivered appreciatively as tendrils of frosty air curled from his lips like cigarette smoke. With barely a raise of his hand, he signaled a passing taxicab.

"I know it's not that far a walk, but I'd rather ride if you don't mind."

He wouldn't get an argument from her. Not tonight. The temperature had to be twenty degrees colder than the night before.

A gust of hot air greeted her legs as Arianna slid across the seat. The heat felt so good, she immediately kicked off her heels and wriggled her toes in front of the floor vent. She'd thought she was prepared for late November in New York, but apparently not. Max's coat, chilled from their short time in the cold, brushed her legs, each feathery touch leaving a trail of goose bumps.

"I'm going to go out on a limb and guess it doesn't get cold on your island," he remarked.

"Not this cold, no."

"Well, hopefully whatever it is you need to sort out won't take too long, and you'll be back to warm weather."

"I was under the impression we weren't going to talk about it anymore."

"Did we say that?" he asked, his grin lighting the darkness. Whether or not he could see her expression, Arianna frowned anyway. "Fine," he said. His coat brushed her leg again as he settled back into the seat. "We'll drop the subject. After I say one more thing…"

Before she could argue, he held up a hand. "You would have made a far better chanteuse than Shirley ever was."

Maybe sitting in the darkness was a good thing since it kept him from seeing how pink she blushed over the compliment. "Thank you." Then, because her conscience twinged over saying no, she added, "I'm sorry you needed to find a replacement."

"So am I," he said, his sigh heavy with regret. "But as Darius loves to tell me, you can't save the world."

"What happened to her? If it is all right for me to ask."

"She got arrested trying to sell drugs in Washington Square Park."

"That's awful." When Max said the woman couldn't fulfill her contract, she assumed there'd been some type of dispute or perhaps an illness. But drugs? Was that what he meant by being unable to save the world?

"I really thought she had her demons beat, too," he replied, "but her boyfriend must have dragged her back in."

"Perhaps now that she has been arrested, she will get some help."

"Maybe. At least she'll be away from her crackhead boyfriend. Then again," he said with a sigh, "who knows? Maybe she'll get out and go right back to him."

She could hear in his voice how heavily the failure weighed on him. Arianna wished she could ease his frustration. "At least you tried to help her," she offered. "There's that."

"Would have been better if I'd succeeded." He shifted in his seat again, and while his voice sounded far away, every move brought his body closer. "For the life of me," he continued, "I'll never understand why women insist on staying with losers when they know it'll kill them."

"People do foolish things when they're in love." Or think they are.

"Suppose so," he replied, his voice oddly flat. "All the more reason to avoid ever falling in love in the first place. All it does is cause trouble."

As good an argument as any. Perhaps, then, marriage to Manolo wouldn't be as awful as she thought. Since she didn't love him, his infidelity and duplicitousness wouldn't break her heart.

"Sounds like a lonely way to go through life," she said out loud.

"You say lonely, I say smart."

"You make it sound like love affairs never end happily."

"Have you seen one that ended well?"

"My parents were happy. And my brother and his wife. Very much so." Father's face would light up like the sun whenever Mama walked into a room.

"You said *were*."

"My mother and sister-in-law have both passed away."

"So they didn't end well."

No, they had not. Both men still mourned their losses deeply. Both of them spent their days cloaked in sadness. In fact, the only time she could remember Father showing any type of true joy was when she began dating Manolo.

Her insides suddenly felt hollow. Settling back into the shadows, Arianna trained her attention on the world passing outside her window. Times Square, normally bright and colorful, was extra festive thanks to the giant holiday billboards and white lights. Seeing such merriness cheered her slightly. "Everything looks prettier at Christmas," she said.

"Wait until they light the tree later this week," Max said as they were passing Rockefeller Center. "That's when the decorations really kick into high gear."

The famous tree stood like a towering shadow amid the brightness. "I'm looking forward to it. I've seen photographs, but never the real thing. The one we have at home isn't quite as tall."

"Not too many trees are, unless you live in a mansion."

Or a palace. Arianna bit her lip. "Do you decorate the Fox Club?" Considering how much attention he'd paid to period details, she was curious as to what the place would look like for Christmas.

"Are you kidding? The staff would have my head if we didn't. Day after they light the big one, we light our own tree. Make a party out of it."

"Sounds nice."

He shrugged. "Personally, I'd prefer a professional decorator, but they have fun."

"I always loved decorating the Christmas

tree." When she was little, her parents would have a separate tree in their suite to celebrate the family's private Christmas. The four of them always decorated it themselves, even Father, who insisted he was the only one who could properly align the star on top. This year, her father and Armando would decorate it without her.

And what of Christmas in the future? Would her child's Christmas be filled with love and excitement? Would they be sharing traditions with a man who did not love them, or would they be decorating alone?

"Hey, everything all right?" Max asked.

Arianna blinked back the moisture from her eyes. Goodness, but she was a seesaw of emotions today. Max placed his hand, solid and sure, on her arm. She suddenly wanted to curl even closer, with his arm wrapped tight about her shoulders. What was it about him that his simple presence improved her spirits? "I was feeling nostalgic again, that's all."

"You've been doing that a lot tonight."

"The decorations bring back a lot of memories. Doesn't that ever happen to you during the holidays?"

"Thankfully, no. I'm much too busy focusing on the present to worry about those days."

Thankfully? This was supposed to be a happier subject. Did he not want to remember? Stealing a look at his profile, Arianna tried to picture him as a child, imagining him as a smaller, younger version of the man she saw now.

"Christmas was always a special time for my family," she told him. "When I was a very little girl, my brother, Armando, and I would stay up late on Christmas Eve, hoping to catch Babbo Natale."

"Babbo Natale?"

"Our version of Santa Claus." One of the many traditions Corinthia shared with its Italian neighbor. "Armando and I would watch out for him every Christmas Eve. I was determined to catch him in the act." The two of them would tuck themselves under blankets near the fireplace, flashlights in hand for when he made his appearance.

"Did you? Ever catch him, that is?" Max asked.

"Never," she said with a smile. "No matter how late we managed to stay awake, we always fell asleep before he arrived."

"Sneaky guy."

"What about you?" she asked, curious. She hadn't forgotten his *thankfully* comment from a moment earlier. "Did you ever wait up for Santa?"

"Santa was kind of hit-or-miss in our house. Is that your hotel?"

He pointed ahead to where a pair of police cars were parked, their blue lights flashing, and any follow-up questions Arianna might have had regarding his comment took a backseat. "Why are the police here?"

"Good question. Wait here and I'll find out."

She was too curious to wait. When Max opened the door, she climbed out after him. "I am the one staying here," she said when he shot her a look.

A policeman stood guard at the front door, his heavy blue coat seeming to swallow him whole. When he saw them approaching, he stepped into their path. "Sorry," he said, his breath heavy with the smells of coffee and cigarettes, "but you can't go in."

"But I'm staying here," Arianna replied. "Can't I go up to my room?"

The officer looked them both up and down.

"You are?" She wasn't sure what was more incredulous, his voice or his expression. "You might want to find a different hotel."

"Why? What happened?" Max asked.

"One of the guests was attacked in their room."

Immediately Max shot her a look. Arianna ignored him. She didn't need to see his eyes to hear the silent "I told you so" hanging between them.

"How?" she asked. Surely when he said "attacked" he meant by a fellow guest. Someone staying in the room.

"From the looks of things, they kicked in the door."

Kicked in the door... He was exaggerating, right? "What about security? Why did they not stop them?"

"What security? We're not talking five stars here. She just left in an ambulance," he said to Max. "You'll be able to go in as soon as they're done processing the scene. Although, honestly, I would consider someplace else if I were you." Arianna didn't miss the way the policeman's gaze slid to her as he said the last part.

"Don't have to tell us twice," Max replied. "Come along, Arianna."

Trailing behind him was becoming a habit as, once again, Max took hold of her hand and led her away. At least this time, she matched his long stride immediately. "What are you doing?"

"You don't think I'm letting you stay at that place now, do you?"

She didn't know he'd been given the authority to *let* her do anything. "I can't afford to stay anywhere else."

"You let me worry about that."

Except it wasn't his job to worry, was it? Or his decision.

Yanking her hand free, she stopped in her tracks, arms folded across her chest. "I appreciate the concern, Mr. Brown, but don't you think that where I sleep is my business?"

"Are you…?"

Whatever he intended to say, he bit the words back and took a deep breath. "Did you miss the part where the cop said *she* left in an ambulance?"

"Of course not. I heard him." It scared her half to death, too, the idea of being alone in her room while there was an attacker on the loose. If she hadn't been able to sleep soundly before, there was no way she would sleep at all now.

"Then why are you being stubborn?"

Because she had been tossed around by circumstance enough these past few days and needed to keep some tiny bit of control over her life, that was why. "Surely, whoever did this isn't coming back. I mean, the police are standing guard…"

"Sweetheart, you don't think that cop is going to stay, do you?" He flashed her an indulgent look that, under different circumstances, would have infuriated her. Unfortunately, she was too unnerved by his comment to be angry. "They might do that where you come from, but here, the police are way too busy to stick around longer than necessary."

Where she came from, there wouldn't be an attacker. He would be stopped by security before he even entered the building.

But this was New York, and here she lived in a cheap hotel where men kicked in doors. Looking around, she saw a small gap between cars, and wedged herself onto the curb.

"Hey, buddy," she heard the taxi driver say, "are you coming or going?"

"Give us a minute, will ya?" Max replied.

A second later, she felt his warm body wedging itself into the space next to her.

They sat so close that Arianna thought he might wrap an arm around her shoulders. Looking over, though, she saw he had both arms tucked awkwardly between his long legs. Like a perfect gentleman. Although it shouldn't have, the thought left her feeling even more tired.

"You think I am being a stubborn brat, don't you?" she said.

"What I think is that you're tired and not thinking straight. Plus…" He straightened his legs with a groan. "I'm guessing circumstances make trusting strangers difficult."

"I trust you," she replied. Strange as it sounded.

"If that's the case, then let me take you to stay somewhere else. At least, for tonight. I'll sleep a lot better knowing you're somewhere safe."

Arianna looked down at her lap. She *was* being a child. It wasn't only about her anymore. She had another life to think of.

And she was tired. So very, very tired. "I would like a good night's sleep," she said, shoulders sagging.

"Same here. So, what do you say?" The narrow space must have gotten to be too much, because he stood up and offered his hands. "How about we tuck you in someplace safe, so we can both sleep soundly."

Why not? She was too tired to argue. Without his body pressed against hers, she felt cold and empty.

Letting out a sigh, she took his hands. "Just not someplace too expensive," she said, struggling to her feet. "I'm staying here for a reason."

"Oh, don't worry." He was already guiding her toward the taxi. "This place won't cost you a penny."

Arianna stiffened. What did he mean, it wouldn't cost her anything? "Why is that? Where are we going?"

Good thing he was holding her hands, because otherwise she would have slapped the smile off his matinee-idol face. "My apartment."

CHAPTER FOUR

"See? Isn't this better than a hotel?" Having punched in the security code on the keypad, Max turned to see Arianna's reaction.

It'd taken some effort to convince her his intentions were honorable. Thankfully he'd been holding her hands when he'd announced his plan, because based on the way Arianna's eyes flashed, she'd wanted to clock him. Even after he explained that it was too late at night to look for a suitable hotel, her eyes had remained suspicious.

He could understand why.

Thing was, he hadn't told her the entire truth. Of course they could find a suitable room, but he wasn't comfortable with her spending tonight in a hotel, period. When that cop said someone had been attacked, his brain ran through every concern he'd had since she'd told him during her interview where she was staying. Instantly, he'd pictured her being carried to that ambulance, her delicate face covered with bruises. With that kind of image in his head, how was he supposed to then take her to another hotel? He didn't care if it was the St. Regis itself; she'd still be checking in alone in the middle of the night.

He wanted her with him. Where he could keep an eye on her. And okay, maybe take things a little further, if Arianna wanted the same. After all, it had been a long cab ride, with her body sliding up against his every time they turned a corner. He had barely recovered from sitting next to her on the curb.

So, while some vein of compassion might have suggested the arrangement, the male part of him longed to take advantage.

Arianna was surveying her surroundings. While he'd been punching the keypad, she'd walked from the foyer into the living room, stopping at the sectional sofa. Yesterday's suit jacket lay draped over the back from when he shucked it off, along with his shoes, which lay on the floor nearby. This morning's coffee and newspaper sat on the coffee table. "Sorry. I wasn't..."

Why was he apologizing? His penthouse

was one of the most impressive ones in the city. What were a few pieces of clutter? "The spare bedroom is behind the kitchen. You should find spare toothbrushes and things in the bathroom."

"Do you host a lot of overnight guests?" The suspicion had moved from her eyes to her voice as she stepped around the sofa to look through the windows lining his back wall.

"Not in that bedroom." He couldn't help but flash a grin when she glanced over her shoulder. They both knew exactly what he meant. "Anyway, I've only had the place about nineteen months." A birthday gift to himself. The culmination of years of blood, sweat and tears, not all of which had been his.

"It's lovely. Especially the view." In the distance, the tower lights on the Empire State Building glowed Christmas red and green.

"That's one of the things that sold me on the place," he said, joining her at the window. "The windows and deck wrap around three walls so you see practically all of Manhattan. There's a lap pool on the terrace as well. It's closed up for the season, but in the summer it feels like you're swimming on top of the world."

"I imagine it does."

The tone of her voice, casual and blasé, made him feel like a bragging idiot. None of this was out of the ordinary for her, was it? Not the million-dollar penthouse or the breathtaking view. With all the business about the Dunphy, he'd forgotten, but seeing her now, he realized how overwhelmingly natural she looked amid the luxury. It startled him, and raised a million questions, not the least of which was why a beautiful woman so obviously from a world of breeding and wealth would want to leave that world? She said she wasn't in trouble? Stupid him for dropping the subject earlier.

He watched as she took in the view, mesmerized by her profile. Despite her pallid skin and the dark hollows beneath her eyes, she remained the most captivating woman he'd ever seen. The way she stood, head high with near-regal bearing, inspired a kind of reverence in him. That had to be why he wasn't peeling her coat from her shoulders.

Instead, he found himself moving toward his kitchen. "Go ahead and make yourself comfortable. I'm going to grab a drink. You want one? Beer? Wine? Herbal tea?"

"You keep herbal tea here?"

"Don't sound so surprised. I'm in the restaurant business. We spend our lives anticipating guests' needs." Actually, the tea was something he'd grabbed at the last minute when he'd cooked dinner for a yoga instructor, thinking a woman into meditation and Zen wasn't the caffeine type.

He found the tin pushed to the back of a kitchen cabinet. A little dusty but unopened. Apparently he and the yoga instructor never got to dessert. "It's something called Moroccan mint," he called out. "Will that do?"

"Wonderfully," she called back. "I love mint."

"See? Anticipating guests' needs." Although, from the way her enthusiasm sent pleasure rippling through him, you'd think he'd delivered on a promise to give her the moon.

"I would have taken any flavor so long as it was not chamomile." Her answer sounded unexpectedly close, causing him to nearly drop the teakettle. Looking behind him, he saw that she'd moved to the island that separated the kitchen from the rest of the living space. She'd shed her coat as well as her shoes, if the height the marble countertop reached on her was any indication. Her uniform looked more like a cocktail dress than ever, the shiny fabric blacker next to the white marble.

Or was the marble whiter because of the black?

Realizing he was staring, he turned back to the stovetop. "Bad memories?" he asked, turning on the flame. She'd been drinking chamomile when she got sick the other day.

"I seem to have developed a dislike of the smell. Mint is far more soothing."

"If you say so. Personally, I'd rather a nice cold beer." To prove his point, he reached under the island to take a bottle from the built-in cooler. "Do you mind?"

"Not at all."

Good, because he needed a drink. Popping the cap, he tilted his head to let the cold liquid run down his throat. Slowly, his insides relaxed.

A part of him felt uncomfortable, enjoying the occasional drink the way he did. With every bottle or glass, he had to remind himself that he wasn't the old man. That a drink did not a drunk make.

Tonight was one of those nights when he had to remind himself twice. All that talk about Shirley and the stupid things people did for love.

It'd been callous of him, pointing out that her parents' marriage ended as unhappily as all the others. He'd spoken the truth, though, hadn't he? Sooner or later "true love" kicked you in the teeth. If you were lucky, the person simply died and left you alone. The unlucky ones got to stick around for twenty, twenty-five years before a heart attack set them free.

So why bother, right?

"I think I see where you got the idea for the Fox Club," Arianna said. While he'd been lost in thought, she'd left the kitchen island and walked to the opposite wall, where his vintage film noir posters were hung. Her swanlike neck curving as she looked closer at his favorite, *Call Her Murder*, a 1940s movie about a murderous femme fatale that showed the killer lounging like a cat in a blue evening gown beneath the title.

"Or did owning the Fox Club inspire buying these?"

"A little bit of both. The movies inspired the club. The club financed buying originals." He took another drink. "You know, a lot of people thought I was crazy when I first opened the club."

Too risky, they'd said. Opening a high-end restaurant during a recession. Who would want to eat in a club that looks like it's from the 1940s?

"I owned a stake in a bunch of bars that were considered sure things as far as income. I got a lot of 'a bird in the hand is worth two in the bush' kind of lectures." Presented in a far coarser way, of course. Definitely too coarse for a woman like Arianna.

"Looking around, I would say you proved them wrong."

"That I did." She didn't know the whole story by half. About all the years he worked in dive bars and sleazy surroundings before finally breaking free. Self-reliance. Now *that* was something worth fighting for. He smiled, allowing himself a moment of self-satisfaction.

Meanwhile, Arianna had turned her attention back to the posters, leaving him to study the way her dress drew to a *V* between her shoulder blades. As his eyes traced a path downward, he mentally counted the knobs of her spine like they were pearls on a string.

What he wouldn't give to run his finger over each tiny bump.

"What made you pick detective movies?" she asked.

"Not detective movies—*film noir*."

"There's a difference?"

"Absolutely. Film noir is a very specific kind of detective movie. Much darker. More cynical." The door having been opened, his inner film geek stepped out. "And they have a lot more style."

"You studied film."

"I wouldn't exactly call what I did studying."

A high-pitched whistle cut him off. Turning off the burner, he poured the water into the waiting mug and carried it out into foyer.

"There was a library not far from our apartment when I was a kid. They played old movies every Saturday afternoon," he said, handing over the cup. Their fingers tangled as he transferred custody of the handle, and he felt the heat swirl around his stomach again.

"I used to go there to hang out," he explained, trying hard not to focus on the way her lips puckered when she blew at the steam. "Or rather, my mother used to send me there to hang out."

"Why? Was she trying to get you to study more?"

"More like keeping me away." Her futile attempt to shield him from reality. In spite of himself, he let out a sigh. "My father liked a quiet house, so the less things there were to set him off the better."

As if anything his mother could do made a difference. The old man inevitably exploded whether Max was in the apartment or not.

"I'm sorry."

"S'all right. I didn't like being around him, either. No one did."

No one but Mom, that was. He took another drink so he wouldn't have to see the pity in Arianna's eyes. Amazing that he said anything at all. Usually if a guest asked about the movie posters, he said he liked detective movies and moved on. His past—especially anything to do with his rat of a father—was best left there.

And yet twice tonight he'd made reference to what his childhood had been like. What Arianna would think if she knew the whole story? If he told her how when he came home from the movies, his mother would pretend everything was normal, as if her hair wasn't mussed and her eyes weren't rimmed red. Would she look at him the same way if she knew he came from a world that was cheap and violent as the movies he used to escape it?

Pushing down the heat threatening his cheeks, he walked into the living room. "Anyway, I used to sneak into the room where they were screening the movie so I could sleep without some librarian bugging me. One afternoon, I couldn't sleep, so I watched. Some kind of shoot-out, pretty lame as far as gun battles go, but I couldn't stop watching. After that, I started staying awake."

"And a fan was born."

"What can I say? They sucked me in," he replied, flopping back on his sofa. Stretching his legs out on the coffee table, he let his head lie back against the soft leather cushion and remembered how it felt, sitting in the dark, lost in a world of grit and mystery.

"Sometimes, I wonder if it was the movies themselves or just being able to lose myself in someone else's story that hooked me. Who knows, maybe if they'd been showing foreign films, I'd have opened a French restaurant."

"Or a cabaret if they had shown musicals?"

Arianna took a seat on the cushion next to him and smiled.

"Exactly," he replied, smiling back. All of a sudden he was feeling quite relaxed. The alcohol was going to his head.

Why else would he be sharing stories he spent most of his time trying to forget?

"I'm glad they weren't. Showing musicals, that is," Arianna said. "I might have ended up applying for a job in the chorus line instead of waiting tables and that would have been a true disaster," she added, before taking a drink.

"Oh, I don't know. I bet you'd have made a great chorus girl," Max replied. He forced himself not to look at her legs as he said so. "We already know you can play the piano. And sing." Granted, she wasn't so great that record producers would be banging down her door, but her throaty voice made you want to hear more.

What he'd like right now was to see more. More leg. More of that gorgeous expanse between her collarbones. Giving in to temptation, he traced the length of her with his eyes, only to discover the dress had too much material to give him the view he craved. The skirt spread across the seat cushion like a black satin tarp, covering her legs down to the ankles. He found himself itching for even the tiniest of peeks.

Making matters worse, she insisted on perching on the edge of the cushion, poised to take flight at any moment.

"You know," he said, slipping a fraction closer "it's all right to sit back and relax. I don't bite, I promise."

"Forgive me if I question the sincerity of a man whose guest bedroom has never been used before."

Gaze shifting to his lap, he scrubbed the warmth from the back of his neck. She had him there. "Well, you have my word I will be on my best behavior." The words *unless you ask otherwise* fell silently at the end of the sentence.

Silent or not, she picked up on the postscript, and narrowed her eyes. "Why do I think you say that to everyone who visits your apartment?"

"In your case, it's true."

"Is it?"

"Yeah, it is," he said, the depth of his sincerity surprising him. "I know you didn't plan on staying here tonight, and that you only came because I twisted your arm."

"Thank you for realizing that."

Those weren't the only reasons, though. The women he usually brought home were all beautiful, desirable and completely interchangeable. One blended into another in an unmemorable, indistinct kind of way. Arianna, on the other hand...

"You're different."

"I beg your pardon?"

"Different," Max repeated. Having said the word out loud, he decided to plunge on with his explanation. Surely he wasn't telling her anything she didn't know already. "You're not like the other women I know. You're..." *A lady*, he almost said. "A cut above."

"A cut above what?" She laughed. A light and airy sound, like bubbles rising up from her chest. It wrapped around his insides, making him regret the promise he'd just made.

"Everything," he replied.

Arianna knew that tone of voice. Gentle yet seductive. Manolo used to use the same voice whenever he was trying to be romantic. Max, however, didn't have to try. The tone came naturally.

Making him all the more seductive, despite his promises.

Setting her tea on the coffee table, she turned to face him only to realize how closely they were sitting when their knees bumped. Quickly, she shifted backward. "Why are you doing all this?" she asked him.

"Doing what?"

Looking innocent didn't come naturally to him. "This. Being nice to me. Opening your home to me." If not to seduce her, then what was his motive? "Why are you doing all this for someone you barely know?"

"I thought we covered this earlier, at the restaurant."

Yes, they had. He'd told her he was a sucker for a sob story. Was that truly the only reason? Was helping her simply another one of his attempts to save the world? It all seemed too good to be true.

She smoothed the wrinkles from her skirt. "How do you know I'm not a murderer like the woman on your poster?"

"Wouldn't that be priceless," he said with

a laugh. "Killed by my own obsession. How film noir."

"I'm serious. You don't know."

"No, I don't. But my gut tells me I'm pretty safe."

Much as she hated to admit it, she trusted him, too. She started to reach for her tea, then changed her mind. Normally mint settled her stomach, but her insides were as squirrelly as ever. "I've never been very good when it comes to intuition," she said.

"Put your faith in the wrong person, did you?"

"More like I didn't trust myself. I let myself be swayed by other people's opinions, when I should have listened to the voice in my head."

"Happens," Max said. "Some people can be very persuasive."

Present company included. "Especially when all you want is to make them happy."

That was all she wanted, only to fail them by falling out of love and running away. The disappointments would continue, too, no matter what future she chose.

The cushions shifted. Max had switched positions again so that his arm was stretched out along the back of the sofa. If she leaned back, Arianna would find herself nestled in the crook of his shoulder. Protected by his warm presence. The notion was scarily appealing; she sat a little straighter.

Out of the corner of her eye, she saw Max's bottle resting on his thigh, balanced in place by his long index finger. "You know," he said, "I always figured Darius would be the first person to use my guest room. In fact, I'm surprised he hasn't, considering how many times he crashed on my sofa before I moved."

She wondered if the bartender would be upset that she had usurped him. "The two of you are very good friends, aren't you?" It wasn't so much a question as a statement of fact. From the start, she'd recognized that theirs wasn't the usual employee-employer relationship. Their banter reminded her of the way she and Armando would egg each other on when they were kids. "I take it you've known each other a long time."

"Since forever," Max replied. "He used to get his mom to let me crash at their place in high school on nights I didn't want to go home. She used to make this dish with pork and coconut milk that was amazing."

No wonder he and the bartender were so

comfortable with each other. "He still looks out for you, doesn't he?" she said, thinking of the bartender's glares. "He's protective."

"It goes both ways. We've seen each other at our lowest."

How low would that be? How much lower could a person go when they spent their childhood hiding in a library and avoiding home? It was a life she couldn't begin to imagine, and the man next to her had lived it. Made her problems seem very small in comparison. Small and silly.

"Did you know he got me my first job?" Max asked. "Bar-backing at this bar where he and his crew hung out."

The strange term pulled her from her thoughts. "Bar-backing?" she repeated. "What's that?"

"Like being a busboy, only without the glamor. Paid the rent, though, which was what mattered. Anyway, a few years ago, when I heard Darius was out of…that is, back in the city and looking for work, I paid him back by hiring him."

But, according to him, he didn't have a rescue complex. "That was nice of you."

"Nice had nothing to do with it. I owed

him. I wouldn't be here if he hadn't given me my start."

Arianna took a good look at where "here" was. As far as luxury accommodations were concerned, the penthouse was smaller and less opulent than many of the places she'd visited. Certainly when compared to her own home. Nevertheless, the apartment had a unique richness many of the other places lacked. A style. Personality. Max's personality. From the film posters to the Scandinavian furniture, the place reflected its owner's smooth elegance.

That Max lived in style wasn't a surprise. She would have been shocked if he didn't. What did surprise her was learning that he hadn't grown up in such surroundings. The man seemed, to steal one of Manolo's favorite phrases, to the manor born.

"And how did you get here?" she asked.

"You mean, the story of Max Brown's success?"

"Exactly." How did a man go from hiding in the library to living at the top of Manhattan? "Couldn't have been all Darius's doing."

"No, but like I told you, he did get me my start. The rest was a combination of good old-fashioned hard work and a lot of luck," he told her. "Helped that the bar owner took a liking to me. I worked my way up from bar-back to bartender to manager, and eventually saved enough money to buy in to the place. From there, I bought in to another and another."

She hadn't realized. "How many restaurants do you own?"

"Not restaurants. Dives. Places a lady like you wouldn't step foot in."

Considering her current circumstances, his continual labeling of her as a lady amused her. "You mean places like the Dunphy?" she asked, offering a sideways smile.

"Worse. These places made the Dunphy look like the Taj Mahal." Forearms resting on his knees, Max cradled his empty bottle in his hands. "Profitable, though," he said, staring at the label. "Very profitable. And, to answer your question, I owned six. I sold them to finance the Fox Club."

"Your labor of love."

"Yeah," he answered in a soft voice. Arianna waited, curious if there would be more. The faraway expression on his face suggested as much. "I wanted to build something I could be proud of," he said after a moment.

"Some place as far away from those dives as possible."

He smiled. "Can't get further away than 1945, can you?"

"No, you can't," Arianna replied. Although he was trying to sound light, she could see the shadows behind his smile. It wasn't only the dives he'd wanted to escape from, it was reminders of his roots.

"It's no wonder you're proud. You've created something really special. The restaurant, that is." Without thinking, she placed her hand on his leg, only realizing what she'd done when she felt the muscles beneath her fingers stiffen, then relax.

"I like to think so," he replied.

The hairs on her arms started to rise as he transferred his attention from the beer label to the back of her hand. She should pull it away, she knew, but for whatever reason, her brain wouldn't send the message. It was too focused on the roughness of his wool slacks, and the strong thigh beneath. Strength that matched the man's character.

She wanted to tell him she understood how he'd felt. While she wasn't running from as significantly terrible a past, she was facing an unwanted future. Surely the two were a little bit similar?

She didn't tell him, though. Saying anything would only open the door to revealing more, and she wasn't ready to trust her secrets with anyone, not even Max Brown.

Slowly, she lifted her hand. "It's getting late."

"You're right. It's been a long night, too. Let me show you the spare bedroom."

"Thank you." The way her insides lagged at his quick agreement she blamed on fatigue. It'd been a long, eventful day. No doubt she'd be asleep the moment her head hit the pillow.

A thought suddenly stopped her. "All my clothes are at the Dunphy," she said. "I have nothing to sleep in." For that matter, she didn't have anything to wear the next day. They hadn't discussed what she was going to do beyond access to a toothbrush.

"Check the bureau drawer. I've got some old T-shirts stored in there. One of them should fit." He pushed the door wide to reveal fawn-colored walls and a satin-covered queen-size bed. "I hope this is okay."

Okay? After two days of dinge and dust, the pristineness of the room nearly made Arianna weak in the knees. Oh, but to slide into what she knew were soft, clean sheets. Her heart bounced at the thought. "It's wonderful. Thank you."

"You're welcome." The tenderness in his voice, coupled with the gentle softness that had taken up residence in his gray eyes, knocked her off-kilter, as though the ground she was standing on had suddenly shifted.

She reached for the doorframe to keep from swaying forward, swearing as she did that Max was swaying, too. His head appeared to dip ever so slightly. "Arianna…" he whispered.

She should have stepped away. Gone into the bedroom and closed the door. But his slate-colored eyes hovered so close, gray back-lit with dark blue and desire, their slumberous gaze rendering her mute. Before she could think another thought, she rose on tiptoes, her lips parting in welcome.

His mouth slid over hers, and she sighed. Long and loud, as though she'd been holding her breath and only just now remembered how to breathe. He tasted of beer and spices, a taste so exotic and lovely she wanted to taste it forever. Max's hands cradled her face.

His fingers tugged at her chignon, pulling loose the strands. Soft moans punctuated his kisses. Wrapping her arms around his neck, she pressed herself against his length, their bodies fitting together so neatly, it made her head spin.

It wasn't until she felt his hand slide down over her shoulder to rest on her ribs that reality came crashing back. With a cry, she yanked herself from his arms.

There was guilt along with the confusion in his eyes. "I'm—I'm sorry, I thought…" He started to back away. "I'll leave you alone now."

"Max, wait." It wasn't right to let him shoulder the guilt, not when she was the one who initiated the kiss. "It's my fault. I should never have kissed you in the first place."

A rueful smile found its way to his face. "Let me guess—you're married?"

"No, not married." Her hand slid across her abdomen. As much as she'd rather keep her secret, he deserved a true explanation. "Pregnant."

CHAPTER FIVE

PREGNANT? MAX PRESSED his palm to the wall for support. Of all the reasons… He'd thought she might be married, or hiding from a jealous boyfriend, but pregnant?

Suddenly, the pieces started to make sense. The chronic nausea. The herbal teas. *This* was why she was hiding.

She looked as mortified as he felt. "I should have said something before you… I'm sorry."

"No, no, *I'm* the one who should be sorry." What kind of man kisses a pregnant woman like he was on his last breath?

Apparently, *his* kind, since his arms itched to wrap themselves around her again. "I broke my promise. Ten minutes ago I said I wouldn't…"

"Both of us were…"

Yes, they'd both been willing participants, but he was the one who had promised otherwise. It was just that when she looked up at him with those parted red lips, he couldn't help himself. He'd wanted to taste them for days.

Still, she was pregnant? The word refused to leave his brain, as though if he repeated it enough, it would make sense. He looked to her middle, flat and tiny in her dress. "How?" That was a stupid question. "I mean…"

"It's complicated."

"I bet." Ten to one she didn't want to tell him the details, either. Pregnant women didn't run away on a lark. Whatever the reason, he bet it was a doozy. What did she say earlier? About not trusting her instincts?

He was too tired to press for details right now. "It's been a long night," he said. "Get some sleep."

"All right." Her attention focused downward, she stepped into the bedroom, only to step back again. "Max, I—"

He was too tired for the regret in her voice, too. "Good night, Arianna."

Nodding, she disappeared behind the door. Max waited until he heard the latch click before turning around. How quickly circumstances changed. No way he could let her leave the restaurant now, or go back to the

Dunphy. Not when there was a child's wel-
fare in the mix.

Memories of her sighs whispered in his
ear. Jamming his fingers through his hair,
he forced the memories to be silent. No sense
tormenting himself over something that
wouldn't happen again. Best to just shove
aside his thoughts.

He headed into the kitchen, away from Arianna.

Arianna sank onto the bed, no longer en-
thralled by the clean linen. What kind of
woman passionately kisses a man when she is
carrying another man's child? She was going
to be a mother for goodness' sake—mother
to possibly the future king of Corinthia. She
had no business kissing anyone, no matter
how seductive and strong.

At least she came to her senses before circumstances went too far. Tomorrow morning
she would again apologize to Max and explain how she'd been overtired and let pregnancy hormones get the best of her. Then she
would focus her energy on whether or not she
would marry Manolo, as she was supposed
to be doing.

"Don't worry, bambino," she whispered. "I won't let you down anymore."

But as she was slipping out of her dress, her thoughts once again drifted to Max. Her body still trembled from his kiss, a reaction she never had with Manolo. Back then, she'd told herself seeing sparks was nothing more than a myth. If only she had known...

It wasn't more than the sparks that left her longing, though. Being with Max felt so... natural. Beyond feeling like she'd known him forever. When she looked into his eyes tonight, it was as if she were teetering on the edge of something more than mere attraction. Something vast and exciting.

She was playing with fire, that's what she was doing. The last thing she needed was an unwanted attachment to a man who, by his own admission, thought relationships were foolish. She had enough going on without getting her heart involved.

Best that she use her head for once, and keep her distance.

When she stepped from the bedroom the following morning, Max was already sitting at the kitchen island. From the looks of him, he'd been awake a while. Either that, or he woke up looking debonair, which, with him, was a distinct possibility.

He wore a fresh suit, charcoal gray if the pants were any indication, while the sleeves of his white shirt were already rolled to the elbows. Meanwhile, her hair was damp from her shower, and she lacked makeup.

"Sleep all right?" he asked. His eyes remained on his phone screen, last night's warm gaze a thing of the past.

"Very good. You?"

"Fine."

Arianna wondered if he was lying, too. Recalling his shell-shocked expression, she was pretty sure he was.

"There's water in the kettle if you want tea."

"Thank you, but I'd rather... That is, do you mind if I..." She pointed to the stack of buttered toast by his elbow.

He glanced up, then back at his phone. "Help yourself."

"Thank you." They ate in silence, the night before sitting between them like a giant third party. This, she thought, must be what a one-night stand felt like—awkward and stilted.

She missed last night's companionship. The ease with which they'd talked. She supposed that was gone for good now. She'd be but another employee.

Ex-employee, she corrected, stomach dropping. She'd turned down the only job she was qualified for. And having told him she was pregnant…

She set down her toast. "I'm sorry about last night."

"A mistake in judgment. It won't happen again."

He'd said as much last night. She rubbed her hands up and down her thigh, wondering what to say next. "I feel like I owe you some kind of explanation."

"Not really. You don't owe me anything."

Perhaps, but she knew he had to be curious. The question she had to answer was how much she wanted him to know. Lying awake, she realized the most delicate part was already exposed. What would telling him the rest matter? "Like I told you last night, the situation is complicated. I came to New York to sort everything through."

Max nodded. Arianna knew that if she didn't say another word, the subject would end then and there. For some reason, though, she was the one who couldn't let the matter go. "Mano—the father—he doesn't know."

"I gathered as much," Max replied. "I'm guessing you two aren't together anymore."

"Not for a couple months. I'm afraid when he finds out…"

"He'll take the baby away?"

"What? No, not at all. If anything, he'll insist we get married."

"Ah." The strangest shadow covered his profile. A darkness from within. "And you don't want to get married."

"I don't know what I want to do." Her mind was paralyzed when it came to making a decision.

Appetite gone and unable to sit still, she pushed away from the counter. "Manolo, he was a liar and a cheat. More interested in impressing my father than he ever was in loving me."

"Is that what you meant by not trusting your instincts?"

"I tried to tell myself I was imagining things."

The view from his living room was no less spectacular during the day. A thick carpet of clouds lay in front of her feet, with only the weather lights atop the tallest buildings truly visible. Hugging herself, she watched as the vapor moved slowly past, enveloping Max's building along with all the others. That was how she felt. As though she was being overtaken by forces she couldn't control.

"Do you love him?"

She started at the closeness of Max's voice. Looking over her shoulder, she saw him standing a yard away, hands stuffed deep in his pockets. "I tried to," she replied, "but no."

"Then problem solved. You don't marry him."

If only it was that easy. "You don't understand. The baby—"

"Lots of women raise children on their own."

"I'm not most women," she replied, turning her face back to the window. "For one thing, my father would expect me to marry."

"Your father isn't the one having the baby."

"No, but he is the one with the power."

"I don't understand. Who died and made him king?"

Arianna choked back a laugh. Of all the

phrases to use… If he only knew the irony. "My grandfather, for one."

"What are you talking about?"

No sense backing away from the story at this point. "My father is His Majesty Carlos the Fourth, King of Corinthia."

He blinked. "King who of where?"

"Corinthia. It is a small country near Italy. Most people have never heard of it."

"Ri-ight."

He didn't believe her. He was looking at her like she was Mrs. Riderman. "Here. I'll show you." She walked over to the counter, where he'd left his phone. "This," she said, pulling up an image of the Corinthian royal family and shoving the phone in his hand, "is me with my father and my brother, Armando."

It took an eternity, but eventually, he looked up at her. "You look better as a blonde," he said.

Her shoulders relaxed. "I was trying to make myself look as different as possible."

"Yeah, that's not as effective as you think." With that, he stuffed the phone in his pocket and headed toward the kitchen. "I haven't had enough coffee for this. You have any more surprises? Got a hired killer after you? Stole the crown jewels?"

"If I stole the jewels, I wouldn't have needed the job." When he failed to even smile at her joke, she shook her head. "No. That's everything. But now you understand why I was so hesitant to say anything."

"Sweetheart, I'm not sure I understand anything." Grabbing the coffeepot from the burner, he filled his cup to the brim. "A few days ago, I hired a down-on-her-luck waitress. This morning I find out she's a pregnant princess. You tell me how that's supposed to make sense."

When he said it like that, she didn't suppose it did.

Her hunger from before had disappeared, the nausea once again taking up residence, although this time she wasn't sure she could blame morning sickness alone. "Do you mind if I make myself some tea?"

"Be my guest. Or should I be serving you, Your Highness?"

"I can make my own, thank you." Arianna turned on the burner. "I only told you because I thought you deserved a complete explanation. There is no need to treat me any differently than before."

But he already had, backing away when she told him about the baby. How could things not change? She was no longer a down-on-her-luck waitress with whom he could flirt.

That was how it should be, shouldn't it?

Suddenly, she couldn't wait for the water to boil. She needed tea immediately. She looked around for the tea bags. "Where did you put the tea?" she asked.

"I put it back in the cupboard. Hold on." The air behind her warmed as he moved closer. He reached above her, the starched cotton of his shirt making a soft crinkling sound as he stretched. The faint scent of his aftershave drifted toward her, reminding her all too clearly what it felt like to be in his arms. She closed her eyes and inhaled.

"Here you go. Teacup, too." His arm came down, wrapping around her as he set tin and cup on the counter. "Anything else?" He lingered a little longer than necessary, as though to pull her close.

The teakettle whistled. "No," she replied. "I'm fine." Fine, except for the shiver that passed through her when he moved away.

"So who is this Prince Charming? The one your father would want you to marry?"

"His name is Manolo Tutuola. His family's leather goods company is the largest employer in the country. Father adores him." She frowned. "Why do you want to know?"

"Just trying to make sense of everything," he said with a shrug. "Like why you felt the need to dye your hair and hide in a ratty hotel. Seems a little excessive."

"You've never been a princess."

"Last time I looked, no."

From his point of view, her behavior probably did seem extreme. "I wanted to be alone to think. Really alone," she added, before he could say anything. "When you're royalty, that's impossible. Besides the paparazzi, there are guards, assistants, traveling companions. Any trip I took would involve itineraries and schedules. Solitude is not as easy as you would think.

"Then there's my father. If I insisted on being alone, he would want to know why." And coward that she was, she didn't want to have to face him.

In her teacup, the tea seeped from its bag like green smoke. "I've never been able to lie

BARBARA WALLACE 113

to him," she said, watching as the tendrils dissipated. "And the truth…"

"So to avoid disappointing him, you ran away?"

Childish, she knew, but hadn't that been a theme lately? "I left a note saying I needed a few weeks on my own, and that I would be home soon. This…" She gestured around the kitchen, "Joining the Fox Club. They were never part of the plan."

She told him about the pickpocket in Times Square. "I was planning to call home when Darius mentioned the job opening."

"And now here you are."

"Here I am."

Letting out a loud breath, Max left her by the counter and paced his way back to the living room. Talk about a story. Most men, upon hearing all that, would usher her out the door as fast as they could, before the craziness got any worse. Only, she was telling the truth. There was no mistaking that had been her in the photograph she showed him.

Hadn't he known from the start that she was different from other women?

What kind of idiot was this Manolo guy?

A pretty big one from the way she frowned when talking about him. "What did he do? Your boyfriend?" he asked, looking out the windows rather than at her. If he looked at her, he'd be too tempted to stand close. "You said your boyfriend was a liar and a cheat. What did he do?"

"I found a pair of women's panties in his sheets. Another woman's panties."

Definitely an idiot. You don't waste your time playing with rocks when you've got a damned diamond in front of you. Arianna was right to kick him to the curb.

Only she hadn't kicked him completely; she was debating marrying the creep. Turning to look at her, he said, "Surely, your father wouldn't make you marry him. Considering."

He wouldn't be the first father to insist a man step up, a voice in his head argued.

The look she gave him was just as doubtful. "Corinthian tradition is very old and very conservative. There are rules…and expectations regarding my behavior. Prior to marriage."

Prior to marriage? "You mean…?" Arianna nodded. She was expected to be a virgin. "Isn't that pretty archaic?"

"Perhaps, but it is tradition. Normally people wouldn't care, but for me to have a child out of wedlock would cause an incredible scandal. My father would be crushed, and he's already suffered enough sadness these past few years between Mama getting sick, and then losing my sister-in-law. I promised myself I'd never add to that."

"Instead you'll raise a child in a loveless home." Such a wonderful solution. He didn't bother asking whether Manolo would agree to a wedding. Marrying royalty was a terrific business move; didn't take a liar and a cheat to know that.

"I told you, the decision isn't that easy. It's…"

"Complicated, I know."

"It is," she said, coming around the island to join him. "I have a duty to uphold Corinthian tradition."

Maybe, but part of her clearly didn't want to or else why run away to think?

"I also have a duty to do right by my child," she said, reading his mind. "Whatever I decide affects his future."

"No kidding."

"I mean more than psychologically. If I do

not marry Manolo, then this child will forever be the king's *illegitimate* grandchild."

He was missing something. The way she emphasized *illegitimate*?

"Illegitimate children cannot inherit the throne. What right do I have to make that decision for him? For my country?" She looked at him, blue eyes shiny with moisture. "So you see, I have to decide which choice is the lesser of two evils."

Sounded like she'd already made her choice; she simply hadn't accepted her fate. Max's insides ached for her. If the situation was different—if she wasn't out of his reach—he'd close the distance between them and hold her as tightly as possible.

But he couldn't. She either belonged to another man, or if by some miracle she did decide to go against tradition, she was having a child. That involved way too much commitment for a man like him.

Ignoring the tightness in his chest, he took a long sip of coffee. "Well, one thing's for certain," he said when he finished. "There's no way we can let you go back to the Dunphy. Or any other rat hotel for that matter. Not in your condition." All it would take is one push by a careless drunk.

"Does that mean you're going to help me?"

"No, I'm going to kick you out on the street." Her eyes lit up like Christmas lights when he spoke. "Of course I'm going to help you."

"But the restaurant. I thought you didn't want me..."

"We'll work something out." Seeing how he'd nearly dragged her to bed last night, the phrase *didn't want me* wasn't the best choice of words. "In the meantime, we'll stop by the Dunphy to get your belongings and you can unpack them later tonight."

"Unpack? You want me to stay here?"

"Where else would you stay? By now I'm sure your father has figured out where you've gone, and has people checking every hotel in the city." If Max was her father, that's what he would do. "You're not going to get any thinking done if you're looking over your shoulder."

"I can't."

Her fingers brushed her lips. He wasn't supposed to notice, but he did. The same thought was going through his mind. "Look, if it's about last night, you have my word I'll be on my best behavior. For real," he added, trying to catch her eye.

To his relief, she smiled. "It was nice sleeping in a decent bed," she admitted.

"You have my guarantee there will be no police raids in the middle of the night, either. You'll have all the privacy and solitude you want. What do you say?"

"All right. I'll stay."

"Great." He ignored the way his pulse picked up at the news. After all, she would be there only for a couple of weeks. And then she would leave.

Because that's how things worked.

Darius was on the phone taking a reservation when they arrived at the Fox Club later that morning. The first thing he did was drop his attention to the suitcase Max had in his hand.

"Going somewhere?" he asked, once he'd finished the call.

"There was a problem at the Dunphy," Max replied. "Arianna decided to stay somewhere else."

"What a surprise. About the Dunphy, that is." Grabbing the coffeepot from the burner behind the bar, he poured a cup and slid it across the bar in Max's direction. "If you want hot water, you'll have to get it in the kitchen," he said to Arianna.

"Or, you could go to the kitchen for her," Max replied.

The bartender shot him a look. "Why should I?" he asked, lines forming along his dark brow. "Everyone else helps themselves."

"Because I'm asking you to." Normally, he'd let his friend's attitude roll off his back; Darius treated all new hires with the same disrespect. Knowing Arianna's true identity, however, he no longer felt right. Arianna cut off any reply he might have made.

"No need to argue," she told them. "I don't want any tea right now anyway. When I do, I will gladly get it myself. What I would really like to do is get to work, if you don't mind."

"Work? Who you going to play for? The place is empty."

"Arianna is going to help me with the menus for the upcoming holiday parties," he told Darius. Before they'd left his penthouse, they argued over her wanting to earn her keep. Max thought about insisting that her company was compensation enough, but that sounded as though there was more to their arrangement than him providing shelter. Plus, she would have rejected the comment immediately. This was the only compromise he could think of.

"Menus?" Darius's frown grew more pronounced, and with good reason since it was usually his job.

"I've got to have her do something since she can't wait tables," Max replied.

"I thought she was taking Shirley's old job?"

"She doesn't want to."

"Doesn't want—what does that mean? She sucks at everything else, you finally find something she's good at, and you give her a choice? What's going on?"

"You two do realize the lady is standing right here," Arianna interrupted. "There is no need to talk about me in the third person."

"Fine." Darius turned and looked her in the eye. "Why don't you want to play piano?"

"It's complicated." Her eyes darted to Max, wariness darkening the blue. "I am not in a position to be onstage at the moment."

"Oh." It took less than a second for understanding to make its way to Darius's face, as

Max knew it would. After all, the bartender had been around the block enough times to connect the dots. He just forgot himself when he got annoyed. Or, in this case, felt disrespected.

"Oh," Max repeated. He took a drink of coffee. At the rate he was consuming the stuff today, he'd burn a hole in his stomach by dinner. Which, thinking about it, might not be a bad idea. It would give him something to focus on besides the woman next to him.

Who smelled and tasted way too delectable for her own good.

Meanwhile, just because he understood why Arianna wasn't playing the piano didn't mean all was settled with Darius. Max still owed him an apology for yanking the rug out from under him.

"Why don't you go ahead and get settled in my office," he said to Arianna, "and I'll join you in a couple minutes. Darius and I have a few things to go over first."

"Are you sure I shouldn't stay?" She looked back and forth between them. "In case…"

"It won't take long," he assured her. "I just want to talk to him about some supply orders."

"Supply orders," she repeated. She didn't seem sure if she believed him. There was doubt lacing each word.

"Yeah, supply orders. I promise. It won't take long." Hopefully she understood what he was really promising, that her secret would remain safe with him. What he wanted to do was take her hands and really reassure her, but that wouldn't be appropriate seeing how he'd promised to keep his distance. "I'll be there in five minutes."

"So that's how it is now," Darius said, once she was out of earshot. "She's your new right hand?"

"Look, I know you're ticked I gave her part of your job."

"No, hey, I'm cool," he replied, raising his hands in a way that said he clearly wasn't. "I'm the one who told you to get her out of your system. I just need to know if this is going to become a regular habit. 'Cause if you're gonna promote every woman you sleep with, things are going to get awkward real fast."

"It's not like that," Max replied, surprised by the defensiveness in his voice. He wished he could explain to his friend that Arianna was officially off-limits. "Believe it or not, I'm only interested in helping the woman."

"Uh-huh." Leaning over the bar, he nodded at Arianna's suitcase, which sat where Max left it, next to a bar stool. "Out of curiosity, where did your newest employee sleep last night?"

Max's cheeks grew warm.

"I thought so."

"In the spare bedroom." So he could wipe that smug smile off his face. "Nothing happened." Nothing except two whopper revelations and a kiss he couldn't stop thinking about.

Instead of his smile fading, however, Darius let out a laugh. "You are kidding me. Max Brown took a woman home and didn't sleep with her? Let me get the calendar. Someone's got to mark this date down."

Max curled his lip into a sneer. "Very funny. You act like I've never gone out of my way to help someone before. May I remind you you're the one who says I'm always trying to save the world?"

"Save the world, sure. But I've told you from the start, this chick is different. I figured it was because you had the hots for her, but now you tell me she's in the spare bedroom, and she's working in your office planning menus? I don't get it. What's the big deal about this particular woman?"

"She's special." The words came so easily, they scared him. *Special* was another one of those words with implications.

Then again, Arianna was special. She was royalty, for crying out loud. She was carrying the possible king of her country. Of course he would go out of his way to help.

Although that didn't explain why he felt protective of her before he knew her story, or why he was still fighting the urge to hold her in his arms.

"I'm sorry, sir. We don't open for another hour."

At the sound of Darius's voice, Max turned to see who had walked in. The man standing in the doorway was tall and swarthy, with salt-and-pepper hair. He wore a navy blue coat remarkably similar to Arianna's in terms of style and expense. His posture reminded him of Arianna as well. Straight and tall.

Regal.

A chill ran down Max's spine. "He's not here to eat," he told Darius.

"How do you…?"

"May I help you?" He didn't have time for the bartender's questions right now. There was no doubt in his mind this man was looking for Arianna.

The stranger regarded him with an imperious stare. "I am not here to eat," he replied, in a lilting accent similar to Arianna's. "I am Vittorio Mastella, head of security for His Majesty King Carlos of Corinthia."

"King who of where?"

Darius had come around the bar to join him by the door. Max immediately shot him a look.

"How can we help you, Mr. Mastella?" He noticed the man's red tie was dotted with what looked like small black dragons. A similar combination, this time in the shape of the flag, was pinned to his lapel. The Corinthian flag. Max recognized it from the website Arianna showed him.

"I am looking for someone. A young woman. I am wondering if she has been in your establishment recently." Reaching into his breast pocket, the man produced a photograph. It was a cropped version of the one Arianna showed him online, with her hair blond and piled atop her head.

"Have you seen her?" he asked.

For the first time in his life, Max actually thanked God for his years of working the underbelly. It took all his experience to keep from reacting.

"Sorry," he said. "She doesn't look familiar."

Mastella looked over at Darius. Thankfully, the bartender could be trusted to follow Max's lead and had a better poker face. He shook his head. "Nope. Sorry."

"Are you certain?"

Something about the man's stare made the hair on the back of Max's neck stand straighter. He seemed to be fixated on a point past his shoulders. *Where Max's office was located.*

"Positive," he replied, shifting to his left. "I think we'd remember if a gorgeous blonde walked into our place. Wouldn't we, Darius?"

"Yeah, we don't get too many people wearing crowns. Unless you count Mrs. Riderman, but that's only on special occasions."

"I see." If the stranger was listening, Max couldn't tell. The man seemed intent on whatever it was he saw over his shoulder. "Are you going on a trip?"

Dammit. The suitcase. That's what the guy was looking at. "Yes, I am." Hopefully the man didn't notice the catch in his breath before he spoke. "I'm heading to Connecticut right after work."

"Connecticut?"

"It's the next state over," Darius chimed in.

"I have a meeting with a supplier in Hartford first thing in the morning. Figured I'd get a head start. You know, beat the traffic."

"Of course." He sounded about as interested in Max's travel plans as he would a listing of menu ingredients. Returning the photo to his breast pocket, he pulled out a leather card case. Expensive leather. Probably from Manolo's factory. Max fought a sneer.

"I am staying at the St. Regis," Vittorio was saying. "Should you see Princess Arianna, please let me know. It is imperative that I speak with her as soon as possible."

He bet it was imperative. Max pretended to study the card. "Sure thing. I'm sorry we couldn't be of more help."

Vittorio, who was pulling on a pair of leather gloves, barely spared a glance. "On the contrary, you've both been very helpful.

Thank you." Giving a quick nod of his head, he turned on his heel and left.

No sooner did the door shut, than Darius locked on him like a laser. "Princess Arianna?"

"You never heard a thing," Max replied. "Not a single word."

"Including the word *princess*?"

"Especially that word."

"Does that mean you're not going to tell me what's going on?"

Max sighed. He didn't like leaving his friend in the dark, but he'd promised Arianna. "Not my story to tell. Let's just say it's complicated."

"No kidding." The bartender shook his head. "Man, you've gotten involved with some crazy women, but this time... You know what? I take it back. I don't want to know."

"Good." Max headed back toward the office. Arianna had to have heard Vittorio's voice. Hopefully she hadn't tried to bolt through the back door.

As soon as Arianna heard Vittorio's voice, she'd leaped from the chair she was sitting in and wedged herself in the space behind the

FREE Merchandise and a Cash Reward† are 'in the Cards' for you!

Dear Reader,

We're giving away FREE MERCHANDISE and a CASH REWARD!

Seriously, we'd like to reward you for reading this novel by giving you **FREE MERCHANDISE** worth over $20 retail plus a CASH REWARD! And no purchase is necessary!

You see the Jack of Hearts sticker above? Paste that sticker in the box on the Free Merchandise Voucher inside. Return the Voucher today… and we'll send you Free Merchandise plus a Cash Reward!

Thanks again for reading one of our novels—and enjoy your Free Merchandise and Cash Reward with our compliments!

Pam Powers

Pam Powers

P.S. Look inside to see what Free Merchandise is **"in the cards"** for you!

W
e'd like to send you two free books like the one you are enjoying now. Your two books have a combined price of over $10 retail, but they are yours to keep absolutely FREE! We'll even send you 2 wonderful surprise gifts and a Cash Reward†. You can't lose!

REMEMBER: Your Free Merchandise, consisting of **2 Free Books** and **2 Free Gifts**, is worth over $20 retail! Plus we'll send you a **Cash Reward** (it's a dollar) which is really the icing on the cake because it's in addition to your FREE Merchandise! No purchase is necessary, so please send for your Free Merchandise today.

Get TWO FREE GIFTS!
We'll also send you 2 wonderful FREE GIFTS (worth about $10 retail), in addition to your 2 Free books and Cash Reward!

Visit us at:
www.ReaderService.com

▲ Detach card and mail today. No stamp needed. ▲

© 2016 HARLEQUIN ENTERPRISES LIMITED ® and ™ are trademarks owned
and used by the trademark owner and/or its licensee. Printed in the U.S.A.

YOUR FREE MERCHANDISE INCLUDES...

2 FREE Books **AND** 2 FREE Mystery Gifts
PLUS you'll get a Cash Reward†

FREE MERCHANDISE VOUCHER

2 FREE
BOOKS
and
2 FREE
GIFTS

Please send my Free Merchandise, consisting of
2 Free Books and **2 Free Mystery Gifts** PLUS my
Cash Reward. I understand that I am under no
obligation to buy anything, as explained
on the back of this card.

119/319 HDL GLSM

Please Print

FIRST NAME

LAST NAME

ADDRESS

APT.#   CITY

STATE/PROV.   ZIP/POSTAL CODE

NO PURCHASE NECESSARY!

HR-N16-FMC15

▲ If offer card is missing write to: Reader Service, P.O. Box 1867, Buffalo, NY 14240-1867 or visit www.ReaderService.com ▲

BUSINESS REPLY MAIL
FIRST-CLASS MAIL   PERMIT NO. 717   BUFFALO, NY

POSTAGE WILL BE PAID BY ADDRESSEE

READER SERVICE
PO BOX 1867
BUFFALO NY 14240-9952

NO POSTAGE
NECESSARY
IF MAILED
IN THE
UNITED STATES

office door. Thankfully, Max's office was set at enough of an angle that Vittorio shouldn't notice the movement.

She could not believe the head of Corinthian security himself was going door to door looking for her. Knowing Vittorio's sense of order and propriety, he no doubt found the task completely beneath him. On the other hand, his personal involvement made sense. If Father wanted discretion, Vittorio would be the only man he would trust.

Thinking of Father made her insides twist with guilt. Was he angry or worried about her? Both, she imagined. That was how she would feel if it was her child. More weight piled onto her already guilty conscience.

What was she going to do? Choose duty or disgrace?

You already know, a voice whispered.

Did she? All her life, she had come down on the side of duty. Father wanted her to stand in for Mama. Father needed a goodwill ambassador. Father wanted her to date Manolo. Was she destined to choose duty again? If so, then why was she hiding behind a door? Why not step out, show herself to Vittorio and be done with the whole silly scheme?

"You can relax. He's gone now."

The tension seeped from her shoulders. Funny how quickly Max's voice could put her soul at ease. Letting out her breath, she let her head fall back against the wall. "Thank goodness. I cannot believe he walked in while I was sitting in plain view. Do you think she suspects that I am here?"

"Nah." Shaking his head, he planted himself against the edge of the desk, once again demonstrating the natural grace Arianna admired. With his hands stuffed in his pockets and his legs crossed at the ankles, he looked calm and collected. Nothing at all like a man who lied to a Corinthian official. "I'm pretty sure Darius and I chased him off the scent," he said.

"Darius?" Her pulse began to race. "He knows who I am?"

"Don't worry. He won't say anything."

"How can you be so sure?" The bartender had shown only disdain for her. What incentive did he have to keep her secret? Especially in the face of a reward. There would be a reward.

"I told you, we've known each other since we were kids. Darius might be obnoxious at times, but he's loyal to a fault. I told him to keep his mouth shut, and he will."

Arianna wished she could share his confidence. Now two people knew her secret. If Darius chose to tell just one person…

Was all this worrying and subterfuge worth it, simply to have some time to think over a question with an obvious answer? For a couple more weeks of Max's company? The knot that had replaced her heart twisted in her chest at the question.

"This is ridiculous," she said, coming out from her shadows. "I should call Vittorio and let him—"

"No!"

"What?"

Max had straightened to his full height, like a soldier at the ready. "You said you needed a couple weeks."

"That was before…"

Before the voice in her head started gaining strength.

"Before I realized how silly this whole idea was," she said. "I have no business running away from my problems like a child."

"There's nothing childish about wanting to think things through. About making the right choice. What will going back today solve that can't be solved two weeks from now?"

He had a point. Her life would be exactly the same in two weeks or even in a month. It was the intensity of his argument that stirred her thought. Reached inside her and squeezed at the part that wished for a third alternative.

She ran her fingers over the brass gussets that lined the edge of the chair in front of her. "If I didn't know better, I'd say you didn't want me to go." She was only partially teasing.

"It's not about my wanting you to stay or leave," he replied. "It's about you being absolutely sure you know what you're doing. This is your future we're talking about."

Wrong, she thought, hand coming to rest on her belly. Her future was inside her. What was left was to decide what life would be best for the baby. She had a feeling she knew.

"I suppose a few more days wouldn't hurt," she said.

Max's smile was far more animated than she would have expected. "Exactly. You'll stay, you'll take it easy and you'll decide whether or not marrying Manolo is right."

"I hope you're right."

"Trust me." He raised his arm, and for a second Arianna thought he was going to stroke her face, only to watch as he combed through his hair instead. "You'll be glad you stayed."

Would she, though? She wondered as a tremor of disappointment trailed through her. The voice in her head, the one who had all the answers, was telling her staying would only make things more complicated.

Because it knew why she wasn't ready to leave.

CHAPTER SIX

"DID YOU REALLY think you'd get away with it?"

Max recognized the actor's voice soon as he heard it; the movie was one of his favorites.

He didn't expect to come home to it playing on his television set however. Tossing his overcoat over the chair by the door, he walked into his darkened living room, only to stop short at the threshold.

There was a Christmas tree in his window. Four feet high and lit with tiny white lights. Candles, too. A half dozen of them in jars strategically placed around the space. They turned the apartment into a cornucopia of holiday aromas: cinnamon, pine and sugar cookies.

Sitting in the midst of everything, wrapped in a blanket, sat Arianna, her attention glued to the television screen. She had a cup of tea cradled in her hands, the rim hovering by her mouth as if she couldn't tear herself away to take a sip.

Max's chest tightened. They'd been sharing a space for only a few days, yet finding her tucked in the corner of his couch already felt normal.

Frighteningly so.

"You've been busy," he said, finally finding his voice.

She started, then smiled. Max's chest constricted a little more. It was the oddest of sensations. Not desire so much as a kind of warmth wrapping around his center. "When I sent you home early I thought you would get some rest, not decorate."

"There was a man selling them from the back of his truck. I saw them, and decided your apartment could use a little Christmas spirit. The doorman helped me bring it upstairs."

"And the candles?"

"The man was selling those, too. You don't mind, do you?"

In other words, she'd bought herself a load of questionable Christmas goods. Max smiled as he walked over to the tree. "No, I don't mind. Usually, I don't bother. I figure the one at the club is enough."

"I'm afraid it's not very well decorated. I thought the ornaments would go further than they did. If I had known, I would have purchased more candles."

"It's okay. I like the sparseness." He poked a particularly large red ball and watched as it swung back and forth catching the light. It'd been a long time since he'd had any kind of Christmas decoration in his place. Always seemed a bit silly since he spent most of his time at work. This little guy looked like he belonged though.

Much like the woman behind him on the sofa.

It dawned on him she must have spent her entire paycheck, or much of it. Less than a week's worth of hours wasn't much. "You should have told me you wanted to decorate. I would have bought a tree."

"I know, but I wanted to do this myself. To thank you for everything you are doing."

"You didn't have—"

"I told you, *I wanted to*. Consider it an early Christmas present."

Because more than likely she wouldn't be here on Christmas Day. Max swallowed the lump that had all of a sudden stuck in his throat. He was used to being the one who did people kindnesses, not the other way around. "Thank you."

"You are most welcome." There was the sound of rustling behind him, as she shifted position. "I have been thinking that this situation can't be easy on you."

"What? Harboring a princess?" He turned with a smile. "I do it all the time, don't you know."

"I'm serious. I know how much I've disrupted your life this week. Yours and everyone else's at the club. You've been kinder to me than I could ever imagine."

"It's nothing." What else could he say? Truth was, he didn't understand his excessive kindness himself. Since they first met, he'd been trying to figure out what made her different from the other people he helped, so that he seemed willing to do just about anything. He couldn't explain it any more than he could explain the desperate feeling that gripped him when she mentioned leaving.

"You know most people who do as much

as you have expect something in return," she told him.

"How do you know I don't?"

"My gut."

"Ah, so we're listening to that now, are we?"

"Better late than never, right?"

In the darkness, her lilt was more pronounced, giving her voice a husky, come-hither quality that went straight through him. Answering the call, he left the tree and joined her on the sofa. To his delight, she moved a couple inches to give him space, but didn't tuck herself tighter into the corner. He toed off his shoes and stretched his legs across the coffee table. "Interesting choice of movie," he said, pointing to the big screen. "Not that I'm complaining, of course."

"I thought it was going to be a musical. It has the word *Holiday* in the title."

"You could have turned the channel. I'm sure there are more festive programs on, even at this hour of the night." This time of year, every channel had a dancing elf or sappy holiday romance.

"I know, but once I realized what it was, I decided to keep watching. I wanted to see what it was about these movies you found so fascinating."

In other words, she was trying to understand him. Max knew the drill. When a woman started delving into his psyche, it meant she was looking for more than a good time. Usually that was the signal it was time to let her down gently.

So, where were the warning bells? The quickening pulse telling him to pull back?

Maybe it was because he knew Arianna was leaving anyway that her question made him lean back with a smile. "What have you discovered?"

"I don't know yet. This movie is definitely attention-holding."

"I'm sensing a *but* coming."

"It's just that I can't help wondering…" She chewed her lower lip. "Are all of them this… unbelievable?"

"Says the runaway princess sitting on my couch." The way she wrinkled her nose in response made him chuckle.

"I am serious," she continued. "The heroine keeps going back to the husband no matter how many horrible things he's done, including trying to frame her for murder."

"Doesn't sound so unbelievable to me." Probably the most realistic part of the whole movie if you asked him. "You said yourself people do stupid things when they're in love."

"You mean like your pianist friend, Shirley."

"Yeah. Like Shirley. Sticking with a loser even when they know it'll end bad." His gaze drifted back to the Christmas tree. Or like his mother.

He felt Arianna shift closer. Sensing the thoughts he was holding back. Why not say more? She wasn't staying.

"The Christmas before my mother died, she and my father didn't have a tree," he said. "My father told her it was a waste of money. She wouldn't let me buy one for them, either, because she didn't want to tick him off. Instead, she spent the last month of her life in a joyless house."

"I'm sorry."

Max kept his eyes on the tree. He wasn't ready to turn his head in case there was pity to be seen in Arianna's eyes. Wouldn't matter if she sat in the shadows or not, he'd see it.

"That's how it works. No matter how bad he made her life, she stuck it out. Said love meant taking the good with the bad. 'Course in her case, good meant getting through the day without a backhand."

It was a running theme in his neighborhood. His mom. Darius's mom. Mrs. Manning on the first floor. Stand by your man until your loyalty dragged you into an early grave.

"They never should have gotten married in the first place really," he said.

"They must have loved each other once."

"Nah. Only reason my dad proposed was because my grandfather made my dad do the right thing."

"Oh." If it was possible for a word to convey a thousand meanings, that one word did.

"Yeah," he replied softly. "Funny, but as far as I can tell, doing the right thing didn't do any of us any favors."

The two of them sat quietly while his words settled between them. On screen, the heroine and her husband fought for control of his gun. It wouldn't end well for one of them.

"It would be different, you know," Arianna said from her corner. "When—if—I marry Manolo. I wouldn't be ruining his life. If anything, this child is the best thing to ever happen to him."

"Lucky Manolo," he drawled.

She was right, though. Her situation was different than his parents' It involved power, money, tradition—everything that had been absent from their lives. He didn't hear any mention of happiness, though. That didn't change.

Why did the thought of her marrying this man bother him so much anyway? It was of no consequence to him what she did. If anything, maybe a political marriage was a good thing. If neither of them loved each other, then there was little chance one of them would spend their days heartbroken and alone.

Who knew? Maybe one day Arianna would learn to love this Manolo guy. She cared enough to try before. And who's to say the cheating jerk wouldn't change his spots over time as well? God knew, if Max was in his shoes and had a woman like Arianna to come home to he would.

His chest constricted yet again.

"Is your stomach still bothering you?" Max noticed she'd taken up her tea again. The nausea was why he'd sent her home early. She'd begun looking pale and tired shortly after lunch.

"A little," she replied, between sips. "I thought I was feeling better, but it started churning again."

"You've been sick a lot." There it was, that overwhelming desire to protect her coming up again. This time, he welcomed the distraction. Rushing in to solve a problem was a lot easier than dealing with the other thoughts clogging his brain. "Is that normal?"

"From what I read, I believe it is."

"Still, maybe you should see a doctor to make sure."

Her hand came down to rest on her stomach. "I'd like to, but I can't figure out how without identification. I thought perhaps a hospital emergency room…"

But that would mean giving her name, which meant being discovered and heading home before planned. "Leave it to me," he said. "I'll get you an appointment with someone who won't ask questions."

"You will?"

"Sure." Because she was special and he was destined to keep bending over backward for her. "Now, what do you say we dump this gangster film and find some dancing elves?"

She smiled. "Sounds lovely."

Yeah, it did. He reached across her to get the remote from the end table. Their eyes met as he pulled back. Her lips glistened, shiny and bright. Would he ever be able to sit on this couch again without thinking of mint tea? He wondered. The scent had already become a staple in his world. Mint and pine and vanilla cookies. Another lump rose in his throat.

"Thank you again for my Christmas tree," he whispered.

"Thank you for everything," she whispered back.

The words rolled through him, settling somewhere near the center of his chest. Squeezing the remote in his fist, Max prayed Manolo Tutuola appreciated the gift he was getting.

"You do not have to come with me," Arianna said a few days later.

"Actually, unless you want a lot of questions from the front desk, I think I should. I'm not sure how much Carol has told her staff."

"How much have you told Carol?" She

stopped to adjust her scarf before stepping through the door Max was holding. Winter weather had arrived in earnest. November's rawness was gone, replaced by a crisp cold that turned every New Yorker pink-cheeked.

Greeting them with a hearty good-morning, the doorman raised his arm to signal a taxi, only to have Max wave him off. Arianna had already said she wanted to walk, despite the cold. She'd been inside too much lately, and craved the fresh air.

"As little as possible," Max replied in response to her question. "I sort of implied you were here illegally."

"I see." They were on their way to a friend of Max's who'd agreed to examine her "on the down low," as Max put it.

"You'll like her," he continued. "She's smart. Very dedicated to her patients."

As well as very fond of Max to do him such a big favor, she mused. The thought sat sourly on her tongue as she voiced more charitable concerns. "Still, she is taking a risk, is she not? Aren't there rules about these sort of things?"

"If there are, she didn't mention them. Though I think she would have done the favor regardless." He flashed one of his knee-buckling grins. "I can be pretty persuasive when I want to be."

She bet. Arianna didn't want to know any more. Thinking about Max charming her obstetrician made her morning sickness worse.

That she should feel possessive at all was ridiculous. Max had a love life before she arrived, and he would continue to have one when she returned home. Nevertheless, whenever she thought of another woman sharing Max's company, sitting on his sofa, drinking tea in his kitchen, she found herself fighting an overwhelming urge to stake her claim.

The reason why was too scary to contemplate. Her life didn't need another complication.

You mean beyond dragging out your decision so you can spend more time with Max?

"Are you sure you want to walk?" Max asked. "Carol's office is a good fifteen blocks."

"I do. The fresh air feels good. Besides, shouldn't you be cold when you are looking at Christmas decorations?"

To illustrate, she pointed to a store window filled with artificial snowflakes. "Perhaps we can buy more ornaments for your tree."

"I like the tree the way it is decorated."

He'd said as much two nights ago. Buying him a Christmas tree had been a spur-of-the-moment idea. When she'd spotted the man unloading them from his truck, she knew an evergreen was exactly what the apartment needed for Christmas cheer. She hadn't forgotten what Max said about Christmas being hit-or-miss as a child.

She had a feeling she'd remember a lot of things about Max. Such as how he smiled at her differently from the way he smiled at others. His eyes lit up more. Or like how he looked right now with his reddened cheeks and his perfect hair blown askew by the wind. One particularly thick shock of hair lay across his forehead like sloppy bangs. It made him look like the boy Arianna imagined he used to be. Before cynicism took over.

Yes, she would definitely remember Max for a long time.

She dabbed her scarf at the moisture gathering in her eyes. "I think the wind is making my eyes tear."

"Definitely stings when it hits your face, that's for sure. Maybe, if you pulled your scarf higher…"

Or maybe if he put his arm around her shoulders, she thought. In the protective circle of his arm, she wouldn't care what the wind did. Since their kiss, he hadn't touched her at all beyond the casual brush of his hand. There was a moment the other night when they were watching television, when she thought he might, but no, he'd remained a perfect gentleman, taking great pains to avoid physical contact. Even when his arm had been stretched out behind her and she'd shifted close.

He was keeping his promise.

She was the one with the problem. The one longing to toss aside all common sense, curl against him and rest her head over his heart. To pretend for a few hours she was more than the latest person he was trying to help.

"If you're uncomfortable now," Max said when she sniffed away her thoughts, "wait until it starts to snow."

"Snow?"

"Uh-huh. Weren't you listening to the radio this morning? The city is supposed to get two or three inches."

"Really?" The thought of fluffy white snow banks cheered her immediately. "We rarely get snow in Corinthia, and when we do, it melts almost immediately, except at the top of Mount Cornier. Manhattan is lucky."

He laughed. "You might want to ask a few New Yorkers before saying so. Snow isn't so great when it's mid-January and you haven't seen the sun for two weeks."

"But in this case, it means they'll have a white Christmas. I would love one of those."

"You could always stick around for this one."

"Perhaps I will," she replied.

Neither of them was serious. Max was simply making conversation, and Arianna...she could only hide from her decision for so long, despite visions of a snow-filled Christmas Eve in Max's penthouse.

"Do you miss it?" Max asked. "Corinthia?"

Funny question. Wasn't it only a week ago she was wishing she were home in bed waiting on a servant to bring her tea? "A little," she replied. "I love my country very much. And I miss my family. My father. Other things, however, I don't miss at all."

Max made a strangled sound, something between a cough and a snort. He thought she was referring to Manolo.

"Other things," she told him. "Additional things."

"Like what?"

"For one, I do not miss having to sit through father's diplomatic dinner parties."

"Bad?" Max asked.

"Horrible. Do you have any idea what it is like to spend an entire evening listening to people talk about themselves? I would never tell Father, but there are nights when I'd rather put my eye out than listen to one more self-important windbag."

"Why wouldn't you?"

"Put my eye out?" she replied with a laugh. "That would cause a spectacle."

"No, I mean why wouldn't you tell your father how much you hate them?"

"Because…" Because he was her father. "With my mother gone, he needs me to act as his hostess. Besides, it makes him happy to have me there."

For some reason, her response made him look down at his feet. "It makes *him* happy," he repeated with a frown.

"Yes. Very." For a long time, it was one of the few things that did.

"Sounds like that means a lot to you."

She stiffened a little at his tone. What was wrong with wanting to be a good daughter? "Of course it does. He's my father. Did it not mean a lot to you to make your mother happy?"

"That wasn't possible."

Not as long as she'd stayed with his father. Arianna kicked herself for asking the question. At the same time, she knew he *wanted* to make his mother happy. Especially if…

"A month after Mama died, I went to my father's office unannounced," she told him. "He was sobbing. Not crying—sobbing, in agony." She could see him still, with his head in his hands, crying as though his heart had been torn from his chest. "This man—the most powerful man I knew—was broken and there was nothing I could do except be the best daughter possible."

Max nodded. "So that's what you did."

"Yes. I became the consummate princess. And then, when Armando's wife died and everyone was thrown into mourning again…"

"You stepped up even more and started dating Daddy's favorite industrialist?"

"He was thrilled. The entire country was

thrilled." Max still didn't understand, did he? The responsibility that sat on her shoulders. "Corinthia is a small country. It's not like America, where your leader is some person thousands of miles away whom you might never meet. We consider our countrymen to be like our family, and us theirs. When my mother and Christina died, the people mourned as strongly as we did. They needed something positive to focus on as much as my family did."

She looked up at his face, which was frozen in a frown. "Tell me you would not have done the same in my shoes? If there was a chance for you to make your mother smile, even just for a little while, that you would not have taken it?"

"Yes, but…" He shook his head. "Nothing."

"What?" If he had an argument, she wanted to hear it.

"It's just that, despite everything in her life, what would have made my mother the happiest was knowing I was happy. We're here."

He reached around her for the door handle, ending the discussion. Just as well. Arianna wasn't sure how to respond.

* * *

It turned out that, in addition to being a kind person and a respected obstetrician, Dr. Carol Miller was also blonde and statuesque. Arianna spent the entire examination vacillating between appreciating her kindness and hating her guts. It was much too easy to imagine this woman sitting in Max's kitchen. Or in Max's bed for that matter.

Speaking of Max, was it necessary to look that pleased when Dr. Miller greeted them in the lobby? Surely he didn't have to hug the woman for as long as he did.

"Everything looks good, although I'd like to see you on prenatal vitamins," the doctor said, when she finished. "Otherwise, development seems to be right on schedule. Looks like you've been taking care of yourself."

"I have to, don't I?" Arianna replied. "It's not only my health anymore."

"I'm glad to hear you say so. You'd be surprised, but every once in a while we get a patient who insists they don't have to change their lifestyle one little bit, including tossing back a few cocktails every Friday night. Trust me, that little baby in there is going to appreciate the fact you didn't."

Arianna tried to smile. "Do you think he or she could pay me back by not making me so sick to my stomach?" Darn morning sickness had been acting up since Dr. Miller walked out to greet them. As soon as the woman put her arms around Max's shoulders, Arianna felt like she was going to lose her breakfast.

"Max mentioned you were sick a lot. I don't see anything to indicate it's abnormal, though. Some women are simply more prone to morning sickness than others. You should be feeling better soon."

"I hope so," Arianna replied. She'd had enough churning for a lifetime. "Personally, I do not know why they call it morning sickness since I've been sick twenty-four hours a day."

"One of the great mysteries of pregnancy life," the doctor replied. Uncrossing her abnormally long legs, she stood and walked across the exam room. "Lifestyle factors can exacerbate the problem, though. Have you been under any stress lately?"

"A little," Arianna said as she scratched at the seam on the exam table. *Stress* was hardly the right word for the thoughts swirling in her head.

"Well, that won't do you any favors, for sure. Try to take it a little easier if possible."

"I'll try."

The doctor took no notice of her reticence, as she was busy opening the exam room door. "Maribel? Would you bring Mr. Brown back now?"

Arianna immediately propped herself on her elbows. "Why are you calling for Max?"

"Oh, I'm sorry. I figured he would want to be part of this," Dr. Miller replied. She had crossed the exam room yet again, to retrieve what looked like electronic equipment sitting on a wheeled cart. "I have to admit, it was funny hearing him be all papa bear on the phone. I forgot how protective he could get."

"Yes," said Arianna. "He certainly goes above and beyond for his employees."

"Employee?" The doctor frowned. "I'm sorry. I thought the two of you were…"

Together. Arianna's heart leaped at the thought, only to immediately fall hard. "No," she replied. "We are not together. I'm merely someone he's trying to help."

"Wow, I'm sorry. The way he sounded on the phone, I assumed…"

"Assumed what?" Max appeared in the doorway. He looked at her from over the doctor's shoulder. "Is something wrong?"

The probing concern in his eyes made Arianna feel more exposed than the paper gown.

"My mistake. I thought… Never mind." Dr. Miller waved her hand. "You can go back to the waiting room. I'll send Arianna out as soon as she's heard the heartbeat."

"I can hear the heartbeat?" Any embarrassment she felt vanished with a flutter. She could hear her baby? "I didn't think I was far enough along."

"You're just far enough that we should be able to pick up something with the fetal Doppler."

Arianna's pulse stepped up its pace. Her baby's heartbeat. She couldn't believe it. Except for the morning sickness and her clothes feeling a bit snug, she didn't feel all that pregnant. Yet she was about to hear definitive proof there was a life inside her. She looked to Max, who was still standing in the doorway.

"Would you like to stay?" she asked him.

"Me?" His self-assuredness, which she

thought was a permanent fixture, slipped slightly. "I don't think…"

"It's not exactly protocol," Dr. Miller told her.

"Please." Nothing about this appointment fit protocol, so why change now? "I'd like him to hear the heartbeat, too." She couldn't explain why, other than it felt important he share in this moment with her.

"If Max wants to stay," the doctor replied.

"Please?" Arianna repeated, looking him in the eye.

The restaurant owner wore the strangest expression. Fearful, almost. His eyes were wide and distant. "I…"

Cutting off whatever he was about to say, he nodded instead. "Okay, if you want me to."

"Now that that's settled, I'll need you to lie back down," Dr. Miller replied. "Max, you can either stand by the sink or you can step a little closer."

Max opted for the sink, a choice that left Arianna disappointed. While she didn't expect him to hold her hand, she'd hoped he would at least want to stand near her.

At least he was sharing the moment.

Lifting one side of the paper gown, Dr. Miller squirted a dollop of cold gel on her abdomen, before reaching for what looked like a plastic microphone.

"Sometimes it takes a couple minutes to find him or her," she said, pressing the tip into the gel. Arianna held her breath while the doctor moved the device left, then right. Suddenly, she paused the microphone an inch or so above Arianna's pelvic bone. "Hear that?"

A low rapid drumbeat was coming from the machine. "Is that it?" Arianna asked. Dr. Miller nodded.

In a flash everything became a thousand times more real. The baby. Gone was the nebulous concept that she was pregnant. This was a real child, a living breathing being whose heart beat inside her. Tears sprang to her eyes.

"Can you hear?" she asked, looking at Max. It felt incredibly right, sharing this moment with him.

Max's eyes were glassy as well. "Yeah," he croaked. "I can hear. I— Excuse me."

Skin white as a sheet, he rushed from the room.

CHAPTER SEVEN

GRIPPING THE SIDES of the sink, Max stared into it, the sound of running water drowned out by his breathing.

The look on Arianna's face when she'd heard the heartbeat... Pure joy. When she turned to look at him, her eyes radiating with the love she felt for her child, his heart had stopped dead in his chest. And it hit him: they were listening to the heartbeat of a child who, when born, would be as special as its mother.

He wanted to grab her hand then and there, and share this moment with her. As if they were having this baby, she and him. It was such a ridiculous thought, he'd had to get out of there. Clear his head. There was no *them*. No relationship—even if he wanted one.

Someone knocked on the men's room door. "Max? Are you all right?"

"Fine, Carol," he answered with a sigh. "I'll

be right out." Turning off the tap, he dried his face and opened the door.

Carol was leaning against the opposite wall, arms folded across her chest. "Arianna's getting dressed. She'll be out in a moment."

Schooling his features into something close to collected, he smiled. "Great. I'll meet her in the lobby."

As much as he wanted to make his exit, it felt rude not to say something before he left. "Thanks again for seeing her today. I hope I didn't put you in too tight a spot."

"Don't worry about it. I'm glad I could help," she replied. "She's sweet. I can see why you wanted to help her."

"I would help her whether she was sweet or not. It's the least I can do."

"Sure it is." Carol's smile came with a sharp, unreadable expression.

Whatever. Originally, he figured on paying back the favor by suggesting a dinner. If he recalled, Carol had been a fun date. A little too focused on babies for his taste, but good for some smart conversation and laughs. In fact, this would be the perfect time to ask her out, only his plan didn't seem like such a good idea anymore. Every time he looked at her, he would hear the tiny drumbeat of Arianna's baby.

"Well," he said, trying not to sound too abrupt, "I should see if Arianna's made it to the lobby yet..."

Carol's hand stopped him. "Are you sure you're all right? You got pretty pale in there."

"I skipped breakfast, is all. Standing in that stuffy room got to me."

Once again he started to leave, and once again her hand kept him in place. "It's funny," she said. "The entire time we were seeing each other, I can't recall you ever getting as worked up about something as you did just now. Reminded me a lot of the new fathers we get in here."

"I told you, I skipped breakfast." Defensiveness kicked in good and strong, causing him to deny a little more vehemently than necessary. "Trust me, Carol, I'm fine. And I'm not the father of that baby, either."

Although for a moment, he did wonder... what if he was?

It had started snowing by the time their appointment ended. Giant fluffy flakes, straight out of a movie, turned Manhattan into a surreal winter wonderland.

"Isn't it beautiful?" Beside him, Arianna had spread her arms wide and lifted her face to the sky.

"Gorgeous." The flakes dotted her hair and eyelashes. He'd always thought it a cliché when he read how melted snow looked like diamonds, but dammit if it wasn't true. Her eyelashes glittered with them. Like a snow angel.

A snow princess.

Flakes blew into his eyes, blurring his vision and bringing him back to reality. "It's really coming down," he said, brushing the snow from his hair. Snow was sticking to everything, including the street and sidewalk, turning both slick. Everywhere pedestrians were waving at the yellow taxis, trying to catch drivers' attention. Raising a hand, he joined them. "Hopefully we'll be able to get a cab." Visions of Arianna losing her balance and falling filled his head.

Her gloved hands grabbed at his wrist and tugged it down. "Are you kidding?" she replied. "Take a taxi and miss my first American snow? Absolutely not."

He knew she would say something like that. "It's a snowstorm, Arianna. No one walks in this weather."

"I do." Grinning, she draped her scarf over her head, turning it into a gray cashmere veil. "You make it sound as though it is a blizzard. It's beautiful out. The perfect day for walking."

A snowflake melted on his nose. "I wouldn't say perfect."

"Please? This could be my only chance to experience a white Christmas."

Her comment reminded him she would be leaving soon. Back to her real life, and he would be nothing but a fond, distant memory.

That's how life worked, right?

Arianna was still looking at him, her eyes as bright as the lights on a Christmas tree. How could he say no? Besides, if he was going to become a memory he might as well give her a day that was worth remembering. "Sure, but will you at least hold on to my arm in case you slip?"

You would have thought he had given her the Hope Diamond—or replayed the baby's heartbeat—the way she smiled. "If you insist," she said, hooking an arm through his.

Covering her hand with his, Max told himself his insides had not just turned upside down when she touched him.

He took her along Fifth Avenue, where she oohed and aahed over the elaborate window displays, her favorite being an over-the-top animatronic display of the twelve days of Christmas.

"Don't they have Christmas decorations in Corinthia?" he laughed when she forced him to stop at yet another display, this one portraying a Victorian Christmas scene.

"Of course we do, just not on such a grand scale. We are, after all, a small country."

"That's New York for you. When we do things, we do them big."

"In Corinthia, it's more about tradition," she replied.

Sounded like everything in Corinthia was about tradition. After all, wasn't tradition the reason behind her leaving? Keeping his thoughts to himself, he let her continue.

"The castle, of course, is decorated elaborately, as is Corinthia City, but once you move to the outskirts, things look the same as they have for centuries."

"How's that?" he asked.

"Well, for one, there are no outside lights. Instead, the houses decorate their window boxes with boughs of green. Then they place a single candle in the center of each window. The green is supposed to represent life, and the candles the blessings that are to come in the future."

Interesting. He tried to picture the image in his head. Never having been much for fancy Christmases anyway, there was something appealing about simplicity. "Sounds nice."

"Oh, it is. If you drive to the top of Mount Cornier and look out, all you can see are single white lights for miles and miles. It's one of the most beautiful things I've ever seen. No offense to your Manhattan."

"None taken."

She was wrong, though. The most beautiful thing was the look on her face when she described the scene. He loved the way her mouth turned upward when she spoke, in the barest hint of a smile. He wanted to brush her lips with his fingers and let her delight sink into his skin.

What he really wanted to do was to kiss her. To hold her like he had that first night in his apartment and kiss her until he couldn't breathe.

Instead, he pulled her closer, pretending it was to protect her from a pedestrian rushing the opposite way. She leaned close, her cheek pressing against his shoulder. Even with the snow swirling around them, he could smell traces of perfume on her damp scarf. Orange blossom.

"Sounds like I'm going to have to plan a trip to Corinthia," he said as he released her. His body felt the absence immediately, making him wish the sidewalks were more crowded.

But then she turned her smile on him, and he felt better. "Oh, you should! You would love it. The air smells of grapes and ocean, and in the summer the sky is so blue you swear you could swim in it. We call it Corinthian blue."

Like her eyes, he bet. "When I visit, will I get a personal tour from Her Royal Highness?"

"Of course. You'll be a royal guest. You can even bring Darius," she added.

"Darius in a castle? Now, that I'd like to see."

It was a pipe dream. By the time he visited, if ever, she would be married and have a whole new life. He didn't want to think about that right now. Today was about making memories. Good memories.

He took her hand. "Come on," he said. "I've got some even better decorations to show you."

"Only a block farther," he told her.

"I can't believe you won't even give me a hint as to where we are going," Arianna said. Although at the moment, she didn't really care where they went or whether it was close by. She'd heard her child's heartbeat, the snow was falling like in a fairy tale and Max was holding her hand. If only every day could be this magical.

She glanced at the man next to her only to get a playful smirk in response. "Honestly, I would have thought you'd guess by now without one. Guess you're just going to have to wait and see when we get there."

So it was some place she knew? Looking around Fifth Avenue, she couldn't see anything other than storefronts. Beautifully decorated storefronts, but nothing that seemed special enough to warrant a surprise. Wherever he was taking her, if Max thought she would enjoy herself, then she probably would.

How different it was being with Max. When she was seeing Manolo, there had always been a kernel of doubt in the back of her head. Well-warranted, it turned out. With Max, though, she'd trusted him from the very start. He made her feel safe. More than safe—special. In a way that being royalty or rich never could.

She had better enjoy it while she could. A week from now, her time in New York would be nothing more than a memory. She would leave and Max would find a new person to help—to make feel special—while she was relegated to the past. Just another face in a never-ending line of charity cases. If she needed proof, she need only look at how he left the exam room while they were listening to the baby's heartbeat. She yearned to connect with him; he couldn't leave fast enough.

For now, however, they were sharing the day, and she planned to savor every moment. There would be plenty of time to be melancholy later on.

"And, we're here," Max announced. He pointed.

Here, apparently, was a block-sized opening between stores. "You brought me to an alley?"

"Promenade," he amended.

They turned the corner, and Arianna gasped. The promenade, as he'd called it, was a long narrow garden lined with illuminated angels and toy soldiers. Their white lights guided people along a walkway dotted by Christmas trees and plastic candy canes. At the opposite end, barely visible in the snow, Rockefeller Center's famous statue of Prometheus held court by the skating rink. And in front of him stood the Rockefeller tree, a tower of white-tipped branches.

"You did say you wanted to see the tree."

Yes, she had talked about it. In the taxi, the first night he brought her home. Or rather, to his apartment. And he remembered. There weren't words to describe what the gesture meant to her.

"This is a much better view than from 30 Rock."

"It's beautiful," she said, looking up at one of the angels. The decoration's white frame disappeared in the snow, making it look like a collection of daytime stars. "I had no idea."

"In the summer time, the center aisle is a series of reflecting pools," Max said, pointing to the strip of red carpet. "I remember my mom took me here once when I was little and I fell in trying to grab the change from the bottom. I had to ride the train home soaking wet. And worse, she wouldn't let me keep the money."

"Poor baby."

"You have no idea. I had at least twenty-five cents."

Arianna laughed, imagining a childhood Max sitting on a subway car in wet clothes, pouting over his lost quarter. "Striving to be successful even then."

"Hey, don't mock. A quarter is a lot of money to a five-year-old. I could have bought a half a candy bar."

More likely, he would have put it in his piggy bank. A man didn't make himself a millionaire from nothing without a well-ingrained respect for money. She respected that about him. Most of the men in her circle had been born into wealth. To have ample money was a fact they—and she—took for granted. Max, on the other hand, not only understood what it was like to have nothing, but now that he had money he also made a point of helping others.

It made him all the more a man in her book. She wondered if any woman would be lucky enough to win his heart or if he would remain cynical about love for the rest of his life. Seemed wrong. That a man as good as he be without a partner.

Not nearly as wrong, though, as it was to be jealous of a woman who didn't yet exist.

To save herself from her thoughts, Arianna pointed to the pavilion where a lot of activity was taking place around the tree. There were people running back and forth, and what looked like scaffolding being erected. "What is going on there? Do you think something is wrong with the tree?"

"Doubt it," Max replied. "More likely they're getting ready for tonight."

"Tonight?"

"The lighting ceremony. Looks like they're setting up the stage and cameras for the television broadcast. Probably doing a light check, too. Would be pretty embarrassing if the thing didn't light up."

"That happened to my father at the annual palace open house. Someone forgot to connect a switch so only half the tree lit. He laughed it off with a joke about elves, but afterward he was not pleased."

"Imagine if that happened in front of thirty million people."

"I'd rather not," she replied, turning her attention back to the stage. "I hadn't realized the ceremony would be such a spectacle. Can we stay to watch?"

"Afraid I should go to the restaurant. You can go, though. In fact, I could probably make a few calls and get you a spot near the dais so you wouldn't have to stand out in the cold waiting for the show to begin."

"That's all right," she said. "It wouldn't be the same alone." *Without you.* That was what she wanted to say. Everything about today was enhanced by his presence. "I'm sure I'll see it another time, and if I don't… It's only a tree, right?"

"Right." His answer didn't sound as firm as she would have expected, perhaps because he was distracted by something on the platform.

"Wait right here," he said suddenly. "I'll be right back."

"All right. Where are you…?" There was

no sense finishing her question; he'd already jogged away.

Cold without his presence beside her, she wrapped her arms around her midsection and watched as his figure disappeared behind the ice-skating rink. What was he up to? A silhouette that looked like it could be him appeared on the stage, but between the snow and the distance, she couldn't be sure.

Ten minutes later, he returned and announced, "Mission accomplished."

"What mission?"

His eyes had an awfully mischievous sparkle. "Stand right here, just like this…" Moving behind her, he put his hands on her shoulders and turned her toward the stage. "And you'll see in…five, four, three…"

The Christmas tree came to life. Thousands of dancing colored lights sparkling in the snow.

"Merry Christmas, Princess," he whispered warmly in her ear.

Arianna fingers flew to her lips. This was why he had disappeared? She looked over her shoulder to find him smiling down at her. "You asked them to light the Christmas tree?"

"I might have persuaded them to test the lights a little early."

For her. "I can't believe…" The words stuck in her throat, blocked by a floodgate of emotions filling her heart. "Thank you."

"It was nothing. You gave me a tree, now I'm giving you one. Sort of."

Arianna shook her head. "Not nothing." She touched his cheek. The stubble of his five o'clock shadow scratched against her glove, making her wish the weather were warmer so she could feel skin against skin. But she was touching him, and they were standing toe-to-toe in the snow, and that would have to be enough. "It is the perfect ending to the perfect day."

His smile sobered, the playfulness growing tender. "I'm glad," he said, knuckles brushing her cheek in return. Lifting her hand from his face, he pressed a kiss in her palm. "Now you'll have something to remember New York City by."

Remembering New York City wasn't the problem, Arianna thought as she looked back at the tree. It was getting her heart to forget.

CHAPTER EIGHT

THE NEXT NIGHT, the Fox Club celebrated its own tree lighting. Max sat at the bar and watched as his staff sang and drank their way through decorating the restaurant. Usually he joined in the merriment, but this year he had too much on his mind.

What had he been thinking? Romantic walks in the snow, paying guys to light the tree early? All so he could enjoy watching a woman's eyes shine like Christmas lights?

That wasn't like him. As far as he was concerned, romantic gestures led to mistaken impressions. Implying a commitment he wasn't willing to make. Yet with Arianna, the gestures came naturally. He wanted to make her happy. He wanted…

And there was the problem. *He wanted.* He'd wanted yesterday to never end. He wanted circumstances to be different. He wanted Arianna… About the only thing he didn't want was for her to leave. Which was the only thing with any basis in reality.

When had this happened? When did he go from wanting to help a woman out…to wanting the woman herself?

On the other side of the room, Arianna laughed as Darlene chased Javier around the tables with a can of scented aerosol. The sound went straight to his insides, leaving his chest with a funny kind of fullness.

It was the same feeling he'd had hearing her baby's heartbeat.

"Oh, come all ye faithful, with a bough of holly…" Darius suddenly joined him at the bar, his off-key voice drowning out whatever song was playing on the sound system. The bartender wore a scarf of silver garland, and had a red paper ribbon stuck to his curls. Easing himself onto the stool next to Max, he flashed a grin. "Yo! How do you like Santa's Little Helper?"

Max blinked. "Who?"

"The drink, Max. How do you like it?"

"Oh, right." He looked at the red martini concoction sitting on the bar, untouched since

Darius poured it. "Sorry, I've had other things on my mind."

"No kidding." Reaching over, the bartender picked up the drink and downed it in one swallow. "These are going to be a big hit this month," he said. "Put some sugar on the rim and the ladies will eat 'em up."

"Don't you mean drink?" Max muttered.

Darius's raucous laugh was the opposite of Arianna's. "Good one! Glad to know you've still got your sense of humor."

"And you're drunk."

"Possibly. But isn't that what Christmas parties are for?" He followed Max's line of sight, before turning back and setting the glass on the bar. "You know, you can take your eyes off her. She won't disappear."

Max felt his entire face heat. "That obvious, huh?" He supposed it was.

"Like a neon sign," his friend replied. "Look, we totally threw that security guard off the scent. He ain't coming back."

"I hope so."

At least Darius blamed Corinthian security for his obsessiveness and not the fact that Max simply couldn't get Arianna out of his head. Knowing his friend, Darius blamed both, but at least he was being kind in only mentioning the security.

"I know so. By the way, you never did tell me her story."

"Told you, it's not my story to tell." Darlene had twirled a strand of garland on Arianna's head like a crown, causing another ripple of laughter to filter through the room. "Besides, you wouldn't believe it if I did."

"If you say so." In other words, he wouldn't push. That trust was one of the things Max liked about the man. He might talk big, but when push came to shove, he respected Max's privacy. "It's got to be good, though, if she's got you this whipped."

Max whipped his head around. "I'm not—"

"Speak of the devil," Darius said, gesturing with his head. "Nice crown."

Wearing a trio of paper bows stuck to her hair, Arianna gave them both a regal wave as she approached. Seeing how brilliant her smile was, Max's stomach did a backflip. "Darlene and the others have decided to go someplace called Xenon," she announced. "They want to know if you two are interested in going."

Darius was off the bar stool in a flash. "I

am primed and ready. How 'bout you, boss? You up for some dancing?"

Max looked to Arianna, who shook her head. "Maybe next time, Dar."

He should have realized the bartender caught the exchange. Darius looked back and forth between them. "Did you two get married and not tell anyone?"

"Very funny. Someone has to stay back and clean up after you people."

Sliding off his stool, he used retrieving the empty martini glass as an excuse to hide the way his insides reacted to the comment. For the first time, the word didn't generate a wave of cynicism. Instead, his stomach backflipped again.

"Unless you all want to do it tomorrow morning while you're hung over?"

"No way. I will happily give you that pleasure," Darius answered. He started toward the coatroom. "Oh, and just so you know, we're all going to be a little late tomorrow," he called over his shoulder. "So you might have to do the opening yourself."

"Like I don't every year," Max called back.

"They certainly know how to have a good time," Arianna said as the crew filed out a few moments later, Darlene leading them in a conga line.

"Yes, they do," Max replied. "Did you?"

"Very. I think they are starting to forgive my ineptitude. Everyone was very friendly."

"Of course they were. You're easy to like." He adored the way her cheekbones pinked whenever he complimented her. "And they are good people," he added.

"It's obvious they like working here. I think they were disappointed you didn't go with them. You didn't have to stay behind on my account."

"Soon as they get on the dance floor, they'll forget all about me. Besides, I was serious about someone having to clean up." Plus, there was nowhere he'd rather be than with her.

Man, he had it bad.

There was also something he needed to do. His own personal holiday tradition that none of the staff, not even Darius, knew about. He moved around to the back of the bar, taking the glass with him.

Wedging herself into the space beside him, Arianna leaned back, elbows against the bar rail. "The tree looks wonderful, don't you think? It makes the entire club smell like pine."

"I think that might be Darlene's air freshener."

"What about you? Did you have a good time?"

"I always have a good time," he said, setting the glass in the dish bin.

"Every time I looked over, you looked so serious. Is something wrong?"

"Not at all." Only a bunch of emotions he couldn't describe and the knowledge that time was slipping through his fingers every time he looked at her.

The cardboard box was still where he'd stashed it last year, tucked behind the spare napkin caddies. "Ah, found it," he muttered.

"Found what?" He could feel her looking down on the back of his neck, trying to see.

"My lucky tree," he answered. His one sentimental nod to Christmas, or to anything for that matter.

"What do you mean? I thought the tree onstage was your tree."

"Oh, it is. This is to hang *on* the tree." Rising, he set the box on the bar. The red corners had started to tatter, and the white cover had grayed a long time ago. "I'm afraid the box is a little worse for wear these days." He'd snatched it out of a recycling bin a few years ago in an attempt at preservation. What was even more sad was that as bad as the box looked, it was in better shape than the contents.

His palms were sweating a little as he lifted off the cover. When it came down to it, his tree ornament was as ugly as sin. Chunky and dull, with several branch tips missing, it looked more like a green acrylic blob on a string. Anyone in their right mind would laugh themselves silly.

He held it up by the string and held his breath. "Presenting my lucky tree."

Arianna didn't laugh. She simply tilted her head to get a better look. "What makes it lucky?" she asked.

"Well, for starters, it came from the very first bar I ever worked at."

"The place where you bar-backed."

"You remembered the term. Nicely done."

Arianna lifted the ornament from his grasp. "I never would have guessed you to be the sentimental type."

"Normally, I'm not." At least he never

thought himself to be, but the last few days had revealed his hidden emotional side. "This ornament is special, though. It saved my life."

"It did? How? It's a two-inch plastic tree!"

"Remember how I told you the bar was a dive?" She nodded. "That was putting it mildly. It was the kind of place where your feet stuck to the floor. I'd mop up, but I'm pretty sure all I was doing was putting dirty water on top of dirt. And you know how we've got frosted windows? The windows there were frosted, too, but with dirt."

"Eww!"

"Yeah." A woman like her didn't belong within a hundred miles of such a place. "Anyway, my first year, one of the waitresses decided to decorate for Christmas. We didn't have a tree so she hung this thing on one of the window hooks. I think it came attached to a bunch of bubble bath she had or something." He remembered the sound it made clicking against the dirty pane. The bright green had been out of place amid all the dirt. "Wasn't much, but it was something."

"How was it lucky, though?"

"One night while I was cleaning up, I knocked it off the hook. When I kneeled down to pick it up, someone shot out the window."

Arianna gasped. "Shot? With a gun?"

"Uh-huh. If I hadn't been under the table looking for this sucker, who knows what would have happened." Touching his finger to one of the few undamaged branches, he gave the tree a small tap. "It's been my good-luck charm ever since."

"As well it should be." Her hand shook slightly as she lifted the ornament into the light.

It was nothing but a tacky piece of garbage, and yet she was holding it as though it was made of Baccarat crystal.

"Amazing how the small things turn out to be some of the most important," she said. "I'm glad you knocked it over that night. I'd hate to think of a world without a Max Brown in it."

"Oh, I doubt it'd be that much different," he replied, pretending to study the box the ornament came from. A lump had jumped to his throat that he couldn't swallow away, causing his voice to turn gravelly.

"You sell yourself short."

"Not really. I'm just one guy."

"I'm not so sure about that," she said. "I know my life is better."

She smiled, and just like that, the emotions he'd been battling found a name. A big, scary four-letter name that jammed its way into his heart.

He curled his fingers around the hand holding the ornament. "In that case, let's hang it together."

Arianna's pulse skipped. Was he really asking her to share in his personal ritual? She looked down at the tree dangling between their joined hands. "Are you sure?"

"I wouldn't ask if I wasn't."

He was just being kind—that was all. Including her because she was there. He had no idea how the gesture squeezed at her heart.

"Why?" Glutton for punishment that she was, she had to ask.

He shrugged. "Maybe I thought we could both use the luck this year."

"We certainly could." Although something told her all the luck in the world wouldn't be enough to solve her troubles. Not unless it could change reality.

His hand hovered by the small of her back

as they crossed the room, a fitting reminder of the distance between them. While they were together tonight, she could never truly be with him. Would it be so horrible, she wondered, if she pretended for one more day that she wasn't leaving? To freeze time for just a little while longer?

"Where should I hang it?" she asked when they reached the tree.

"I usually hang it in the back, near the top where no one can see. Can you reach?"

"I think so. If I stand on my tiptoes." They were, it appeared, the magic words, because suddenly his hands were on her hips, steadying her. Keeping her safe, as he always did. She looped the ornament over a branch just below the peak. Safe in its new home, the green blob swung back and forth, the plastic catching the overhead light and looking almost decorative.

"What do you think?" she asked.

"Beautiful."

His voice was rough and low, sliding down her spine until it pooled at the base, where it set her insides aching. Turning slowly, she found herself face-to-face with eyes dark with desire. Heavy-lidded, they searched her face, looking for what, she wasn't sure. Permission? She shivered. He needn't look very hard.

"Beautiful," he repeated. Suddenly, his fingers were tracing her jaw. Slow and soft, their path stoked memories of their first kiss. The ache inside her grew stronger. She could feel the vibrations of his breath against her breasts. Shallow and ragged.

His hand moved to the back of her neck. Arianna's eyes fluttered shut. She let her head fall back, baring her neck in silent acquiescence. She felt his breath on her lips and then, the rest of the world vanished as his lips covered hers, his unique, indescribable flavor traveling over her tongue and into her soul. Wrapping her arms around his neck, she returned the kiss as deeply as she could.

Time and reality could wait.

"Arianna!"

Her heart froze. *Father?*

CHAPTER NINE

ARIANNA SPRANG FROM Max's arms, practically
shoving him in an effort to be free before
Father saw her. She couldn't believe he was
here. How did he know where to find her?
A quick look at Max said he was as shocked
as she.

Was it possible she heard wrong? Maybe it
was someone else with an accent that sounded
like Father.

"Is anyone here? I demand you show your-
selves immediately!"

It was definitely Father. Smoothing her
hair, and praying it wasn't too obvious what
she and Max had been up to, Arianna stepped
out from behind the tree.

There, in the middle of the dining room,
surrounded by discarded garlands and plastic cups, stood His Majesty King Carlos IV,
wearing a scowl to beat all scowls.

"I thought you said she was here," he hissed to Vittorio. "Aria—"

She took a deep breath. "Hello, Father."

"Arianna!" The scowl vanished in favor of relief as he rushed to the stage, his arms around her before she could say another word. "Oh, my precious little girl! I'm so glad to see you." He crushed her to him, enveloping her in a ferocious cocoon of wool and fatherly affection.

Arianna closed her eyes. While she'd had bouts of homesickness, she hadn't until this moment realized how much she missed her family. She clung to him just as ferociously, feeling his body tremble with emotion. His coat smelled of nicotine, the aroma sending guilt stabbing through her. He only smoked when he was extremely distraught. "I'm sorry, Father," she murmured against his shoulder. "I didn't mean to make you worry."

She pulled back to see unshed tears glistening in his eyes. "Worry?" he said. "You frightened me half to death."

"Didn't you get my note?"

"You mean that slip of paper telling me you needed a couple weeks alone to 'think'?" He tossed up his hands and made a scoffing sound. "How was *that* supposed to keep me from worrying? When I didn't know where you were or what had happened? I was afraid I'd..."

His words might have drifted off, but Arianna heard them anyway. He was afraid he'd lost her, too. Like her mother and sister-in-law.

Now that she looked closer, she saw how badly the uncertainty had taken a toll. He looked older. Weary. Normally pale, his face looked even gaunter than usual, the bags under his eyes looking more like bruises than circles. It was the same face he'd worn for weeks following Mama's and Christina's deaths. Realizing she was responsible for its return made her sick to her stomach.

"But you found me now," she said, touching his cheek. "I'm all right."

"Thank goodness. And thank goodness Vittorio tracked you down to New York, or I would still be... What did you do to your hair?"

"My...?" Her fingers brushed the ends. Right. Her hair. She'd grown so used to the new color, she'd forgotten.

"I suspect she changed colors so she would

be harder to spot in a crowd," Vittorio replied, with, to her surprise, a hint of admiration.

"But why? Why run away in the first place? Did something happen? You look pale. Are you sick?" He cupped her face, like he used to do when she was little and came to him crying, a tender gesture that only made her feel guiltier.

"No, Father, I'm not sick."

"Then I don't understand? If you needed time to think, why not go to the apartment in Milan or have Sergio take you on the yacht? Why hide yourself in some..." He shook a piece of tinsel from his shoe. "Some common nightclub."

"I beg your pardon. The Fox Club is hardly common."

Max. Distracted as she'd been with her father's appearance, she'd forgotten he was standing behind her. She watched him as he stepped off the stage, the familiar tingle running through her from his presence.

From the way his eyes widened, Father hadn't noticed Max, either. "Who are you?" he asked, in his best dismissive tone.

"Max Brown. I own this establishment."

She heard Vittorio suck in his breath as

Max extended a hand. Royal protocol dictated that commoners wait until the king offered his hand. Doing otherwise was considered not only presumptuous, but a huge breach of decorum.

Her father shook it. Arianna and Vittorio exchanged a look. The last time someone broke protocol, Father stared him down. Either he was too tired to protest, or he actually saw Max as someone worthy of respect. Considering Max's natural air of authority, she liked to think it was the latter.

Especially since Max acted as if shaking hands with royalty was something he did every day. "It's a pleasure to meet you, Your Majesty," he said. "And, nice to see you, too, Mr. Mastella. I wasn't expecting to see you again."

"So I gathered," Vittorio replied. "How was your trip to Connecticut, by the way? The one you planned to take with Princess Arianna's luggage?"

He closed his eyes at the security chief's question, the way someone did when they realized they'd been fooled. "You recognized the suitcase."

"All members of the royal family carry luggage with very specific markings for security purposes. Although I'll admit, you and your friend put on a very entertaining show," he added with a superior smile.

There was regret in Max's eyes as he turned to her. "I'm sorry. I didn't know."

"It's not your fault," she replied. Neither of them could have predicted Vittorio recognizing her suitcase. Nor had she known about the security markings. It was simply a case of bad luck. "Max has been helping me," she told her father.

"By lying to Vittorio." Having been assured of her safety, her father had reverted to his imperial self. He jutted his chin, giving the impression of looking down even though Max was several inches taller. "Forgive me if I do not thank you, Mr. Brown."

"But you should," Arianna said. Heaven knew what Vittorio told him, but it was important that Father knew the kind of man Max was. That he wasn't the bad guy in all this. "You have no idea how much he helped me. Without him, I would have... He went out of his way to make me feel safe," she said, smiling in his direction. "I'm not sure what I would have done without him."

"It was my pleasure."

He smiled back, and it was as though they were back behind the tree, sharing a moment meant for only the two of them.

"If that is true…" Her father's voice interrupted the moment. "Then you have my gratitude, Mr. Brown."

"Like I said, it was my pleasure. Your daughter is a special lady."

"May I remind you to whom you are speaking?" Vittorio looked about to have an aneurysm from the lack of protocol. He took a step forward only to be waved off.

"It's not necessary, Vittorio. I'm sure Mr. Brown means no offense. As for you…" He turned to Arianna. "I trust you are ready to come home?"

The question made her heart ache. She would never be truly ready to leave. Not when her heart wanted to stay in New York. With Max, who was ten times the man Manolo would ever be. But, as she was learning, the heart couldn't always have what it wanted. It was time for her to stop running away and face reality. She pressed a hand to her stomach. Face her responsibilities. And that meant letting Manolo know he was going to be a father, and letting her child grow up with every advantage possible.

It was the decision she knew she'd make all along. She just hadn't wanted to face it.

Shoulders heavy, she nodded. "I have to pick up my belongings." It would give her a chance to see Max's apartment one last night.

"Wait. You're going?" Grabbing her arm, Max turned her around to face him with a force that would have had him pinned to the floor if she hadn't stopped Vittorio with her hand.

Even so, his face looked like it had been slapped, all wild-eyed with disbelief. "Just like that?" he asked. "You're going to go back?"

Surely, he wasn't that surprised. They'd both known her returning to Corinthia was inevitable. "I have to. You know that."

"But what about…?" He looked down to her stomach and back up again. The answer must have shone in her eyes, because his suddenly darkened with remorse. "No."

"It's the right thing to do," Arianna whispered. There was so much more she wanted to say, but with Father standing behind her, she couldn't. Then again, she wondered if her words would have made a difference. From the look on Max's face, she didn't think so, but she tried anyway. "It won't be the same," Arianna added.

"Not the same," he repeated in a rough voice. His jaw was tensed, a tiny muscle twitch revealing precisely how tightly he was clenching his teeth. She waited for him to release her arm. Instead, his grip tightened. "Come with me," he said.

"I don't think…" Without waiting for an answer, Max pulled Arianna across the dining room, and before her father or Vittorio were able to respond, pushed her into the room and closed the door behind them.

As a deterrent, it wasn't the best. If they didn't come back out, Father would only instruct Vittorio to kick the door in. "You do know—" she began.

"Marry me."

Arianna froze where she stood. He did not just ask her to…

"Marry me," Max repeated, this time taking her hands in his. "Tell him I'm the baby's father and marry me."

Marry Max. They were the two most incredible words. In her mind, she could see it all. The three of them. A happy, loving family.

Only, Max didn't say anything about love, did he?

She looked down at their joined hands. Max's grip was solid and warm, like the support he offered. "You want to take Manolo's place?"

"Why not? You said yourself you don't love Manolo. This way you'll be in control. You can please your father and not have to spend your life stuck in a bad marriage."

Of course she wouldn't, because when the time came, Max would no doubt devise a way for them to part amicably. What he was offering was a business partnership complete with an exit strategy. It was an incredibly generous and selfless offer.

"The lesser of two evils," she said flatly.

No need to ask him why. He was stepping up, the way he always did. Trying to save the world, or at least trying to save her from falling into the same hopeless morass as his mother.

Too late, she wanted to tell him. She'd fallen the moment he'd had the tree lit in Rockefeller Center for her. Maybe even before.

"It's the perfect solution," he said, his certainty painful to listen to.

On the contrary, it was no solution at all. Spending a month, a year, married to Max, knowing he'd only agreed out of some overblown sense of nobility? The fantasy of what she wished could be would haunt her forever.

Nor could she do it to him. Tie him to a woman and child that weren't his. She cared for him far too much.

If anyone was going to make a sacrifice in this room, it would be her.

The pounding started on the door. "Your Highness, is everything all right? Do you need help?"

"I'm fine, Vittorio," she called back. "I will be out in a moment." Reluctantly, she pulled her hands free. "We'd best open the door or they will knock it down."

"They better not. That's solid oak." He strode across the room and turned the latch. The tumbler clicked loudly. Vittorio, standing on the other side, had to have heard.

Max pressed a hand against the wood. One hand wouldn't be enough to stop Vittorio entering, but it didn't matter. They only needed a moment; they would be leaving soon enough. "How do you want to tell them?" he asked her.

Her stomach twisted into a knot. "I'm not."

"What?" Door forgotten, Max's hand dropped to his side. "What do you mean?"

"I'm not telling them you're the father," she replied. She couldn't.

A storm flashed behind Max's eyes as they widened in disbelief. What had been cool and gray had become mottled steel and navy. "Why the hell not?" he asked. "I just told you, it's the perfect solution."

Except there was no love. If he would offer but one tiny word to make her believe he cared... Anything at all. It didn't even have to be the word *love*. One word and she would stay with him forever.

But all he had to offer was a business partnership and an exit strategy. It hurt to look him in the eye. She had to turn to his desk. "I cannot keep the truth from Manolo. He has a right to know he is going to be a father."

"Even if he doesn't deserve to be? The child deserves a happy home."

"He will have one. His mother will love him. His grandfather, his uncle. He will be surrounded by love. Besides, people can change. Who is to say fatherhood isn't exactly what Manolo needs? People do grow up." She had. Just now.

"Besides," she added, her fingers tapping out a nervous rhythm on the desktop, "being honest with him is the right thing to do."

"The right thing..." There was a thud, and she realized Max had punched the door. "So that's it? You're just going to walk out of here and marry a man you don't love—who doesn't love you—because it's the right thing."

Better than marrying a man she *did* love who didn't love her. "Yes, I am."

"Unbelievable," he muttered.

Arianna wanted to punch a door herself. She was tired of having this discussion. Max could remind her about Manolo until he was blue in the face, but it wouldn't change anything. She would still be pregnant, and neither man would love her.

"I told you," she said, whirling around. It was the first time she'd looked him in the eye since he'd offered marriage. "The rules are different for people like me. There are traditions, expectations I'm expected to live up to. My father—"

"Your father would want you to be happy," he growled. "How does sacrificing yourself accomplish that? Tell me."

"It doesn't…"

Matter, she was going to say, but Vittorio chose that moment to open the door. Max attempted to push it shut, but the security chief wedged his foot in the space, blocking him.

"Your father is wondering if you're ready to leave. We have a rather long flight ahead of us."

There was certainly nothing more to be said here. At least nothing she could say aloud. Slipping back behind her regal facade, she offered Vittorio a cool and efficient nod. "Of course. I was just leaving."

When she reached the office door, she paused long enough to steal one last memory of Max's movie-star face. The storm still raged in his eyes. "Arianna," he said, trying one last time.

"Goodbye, Max," she replied. "Thank you for everything."

Do not turn around, she told herself as she joined her father. *Do not cast a final glance at the club that you will never forget. Do not think about how soon there will be another desperate soul who needs help, making you a dim memory. Above all, do not let anyone know that leaving the Fox Club is killing you on the inside.*

Head held high, she followed her father out the door.

Max stood shell-shocked, his feet frozen in place. That was it? She was just going to leave? Less than an hour ago the two of them were kissing behind the Christmas tree. The most mind-blowing kiss of his life. And now she was walking out without so much as a look back?

The door closed. The sound of the click reverberating in the empty club did what the sight of her leaving couldn't and that was prod him to move. Rushing to the entrance, he yanked open the door and stepped outside, making it to the sidewalk in time to see the limousine's taillights pulling into the traffic. He stood there in the cold, and his gaze followed the red lights until they became one with a sea of taillights and disappeared into the night.

She was gone.

He could try and intercept her at his apartment, but what good would it do? The woman had made up her mind. Chosen to throw her life away and subject her child to a loveless marriage.

At least he could say that he'd tried. Offered her a chance to please her father and control her destiny.

Why on earth did she reject him?

He didn't want to think about the panic that had spurred him to ask in the first place. The same icy fear that was squeezing his chest right now. The one that felt like the earth was crumbling beneath his feet, leaving him without purchase.

Slowly, he made his way back into the restaurant. Someone had decided to create a display atop the reservation desk. Boughs of evergreen and holly surrounded one of the hurricane candles he'd bought for the dining room. He twisted a branch between his thumb and forefinger.

Green for life; candles for the blessings to come in the future. The tradition of Corinthia.

He'd have Javier remove the greenery tomorrow.

Right now, he needed to clean away the remains of the day. Maybe by the time he had done that, this hollow, off-balance sensation would have faded.

Honestly, he didn't know why he was disturbed in the first place. Arianna's leaving was hardly a surprise; he'd known all along her stay was temporary.

After all, wasn't that how life worked?

The feeling didn't go away. If anything, the sensation worsened until by the following night it had grown to a heavy ache that weighed him down. He couldn't seem to do anything. Paperwork sat on his desk untouched while he stared into space for hours at a time. After a couple of luckless attempts, staff members started going to Darius with questions. And as for going home... He didn't. He thought about it, but then he recalled the image of his Christmas tree in the window, and the inertia would grip him stronger than before.

Shortly after midnight, a knock sounded on his office door and Darius's head appeared. "We're down to just a few tables. I'm going to go ahead and announce last call."

"Sure." His voice sounded as distant as his

thoughts. "What about that paralegal party? They still here?"

"That's tomorrow, boss."

"Sorry. I lost track of the day."

"You've been losing track of a lot today. I'd blame last night's party, but you didn't drink." The bartender stepped inside and closed the door. "Everything all right?"

"Everything's fine," Max replied. "I'm just a little out of it, is all."

"No kidding. I noticed your new roommate isn't around tonight, either. You two have a fight?"

"You could say that." If by fight he meant Arianna walking out. "She's gone."

Darius's jaw dropped. He sat down, wearing a look of confusion. "What do you mean gone? Where'd she go?"

"Home. Back to Corinthia."

"You mean, where that guy the other day was from?"

Max nodded. He thought about sighing, but exhaling seemed like too much work. "That's the place."

"But I thought she didn't want to go back. What happened?"

Max told him about King Carlos. When he

finished, Darius sat back, his jaw lower than before. "An actual king here in the restaurant. So that dude wasn't kidding about Arianna being a princess."

"Nope."

The swear word he muttered under his breath was the same one Max had been mentally repeating since last night.

"Apparently His Majesty decided to retrieve his errant daughter in person."

"Wow." The bartender shook his head. "That sure don't happen every day, not to guys from our neighborhood. You think you might want to tell me the whole story now?"

"Not much more to tell," Max replied. "I didn't know she was a princess until the night she played piano. Before that, I thought she was just another hard-luck case. Turns out she simply wanted a few weeks of anonymity." Some things, like Arianna's pregnancy, still weren't for him to announce. Funny, how he felt honor-bound to keep her secrets, even after she was gone.

He did tell Darius about her being robbed, though, and how she impulsively applied for the job when the bartender mentioned it.

"So, I'm the reason we ended up with her,"

he remarked. "This explains why she sucked as a server. And why she was staying at a pit like the Dunphy, too."

"Yep." Attempting to project an indifference he didn't feel, Max leaned back and perched his legs on the edge of his desk. "And why I had her move into my spare room. Once I figured out she was royalty, I couldn't very well let her go back to that dive." Not when he could come home to her sitting on his sofa. His apartment was going to feel very different now that he was back to living alone.

"So, that's it, huh? She's gone for good?"

"She never planned to stay long to begin with."

"Too bad. She was just beginning to grow on me. You going to be okay?"

"Me? Sure, I'll be fine," he said, waving off the question. Wasn't as though Arianna was the first person to pass through his life. She was just another woman. Another lost puppy. A new one would replace her soon enough.

"You sure?" Darius asked.

"Of course. Why wouldn't I be?"

"I don't know, maybe because you're wearing your emergency suit, which tells me you didn't go home last night."

"I was busy cleaning."

"For twenty-four hours?"

His friend got up and walked around to Max's side of the desk. "Look," he said, "why don't you just admit you had a thing for the lady. Last time I looked, it wasn't a crime."

"Maybe not, but it never did anyone any favors, either. Or have you forgotten what it was like in our neighborhood?"

"That's because the people we grew up with were losers. Or hooked on losers."

"Present company excluded," Max replied automatically.

"Half of it anyway," Darius replied. "You're not like the people in our neighborhood, and Arianna definitely isn't. In fact, she's about as far from our neighborhood as you can get. Like, 'out of this world' far."

"What's your point?" His head was beginning to hurt; the last thing he needed was to be reminded of Arianna's uniqueness.

"My point is… I don't know. I just don't think the world will end if you like her, is all."

Tell that to the hole in his chest. "Well, it doesn't matter now, does it? She's gone."

"What? They don't have phones where she's from? Or email?"

"It's not that simple," Max said. "There are complications."

"These complications have anything to do with the lady being nauseous all the time, and scarfing down saltines from the salad bar?

"I heard the waitresses gossiping," he said when Max failed to hide his surprise. "I wasn't sure if they were being catty or what. Is it true?"

He plucked at the seam on his pants. So much for keeping his end of the bargain. "She didn't want anyone to know."

"Now I get why you backed off. I mean, pregnant with another man's kid? That's some serious baggage. I know I couldn't—"

"I asked her to marry me."

"Say what?" Darius looked at him bug-eyed.

"I told her to tell her father I was the one who got her pregnant and that we would get married."

"What the…? Why would you do that?"

"To give her a choice," Max explained. "So she wouldn't have to go back to Corinthia and marry a man she didn't love." So the light in those beautiful blue eyes wouldn't fade under the weight of disregard.

"Yeah, but to step up when the kid's not even yours?" For the second time in the conversation, Darius swore. "That's brave even for you."

"Doesn't matter. The lady said no." Max could still hear the door clicking as she walked away.

"Of course she did. Getting out of marrying a guy she doesn't love by marrying another guy she doesn't love? Talk about a crazy idea."

"Her father was getting ready to take her away. I had to come up with something to keep her from leaving."

"So you proposed? What would you have done if she actually said yes?"

"What do you mean, what would I have done? I would have married her."

"And spent the rest of your life raising some other dude's kid."

To his surprise, the thought didn't make his pulse race. If anything, his heart grew heavier.

"It wouldn't have been so bad." Max could have given the child everything his father never gave him. Attention, affection. "The three of us could have made a pretty decent family."

But she didn't want it. She'd rather lock herself to a serial adulterer for the rest of her life.

Why? Why wasn't his proposal good enough? He'd been asking himself that question since she walked away. It was the one piece of the puzzle he couldn't figure out, and he was tired of trying to find it. Tired of everything.

He needed a drink. And not a beer, either. He needed something hard enough to silence the thoughts spinning through his head. Like tequila or whiskey. His dad liked Kentucky bourbon. Maybe he should go with that? Take a page from a professional.

"Man, I knew I should have set up a pool." Darius followed him from out of the office and behind the bar. Taking two tumblers off the top shelf, he set them on the counter, then took the bottle from Max's hand. "I called this thing from day one."

"Called what thing?" He pushed the nozzle back toward the glass to keep Darius from pouring.

"You falling for Arianna. Soon as I saw your face, I knew you were a goner."

"I was not." It was a feeble protest, at best.

Darius was right. He had fallen when he saw Arianna. Who wouldn't? She was beautiful, sweet, kind...

Special.

The hole inside his chest ripped open, and all the emotions he'd been pretending didn't exist came pouring out. Years of telling himself love was a waste of time and what happened? He fell anyway. Hard.

Thing was, in the end, he was right anyway. The only thing falling in love did for him was make Arianna's departure ten times worse.

Groaning, he banged his head against the shelves. "I'm an idiot."

"I take it that's your way of saying you got feelings for this woman."

Feelings? They were talking way more than just feelings. "I love her." As soon as he said the words, he knew he meant them. He loved Arianna. "What am I going to do?"

After he got good and drunk, that was. How would he ever feel complete again?

Darius handed him a drink. "Does she know how you feel?"

"I asked the woman to marry me."

"Yeah, but did you tell her *why* you wanted to marry her?"

"No." So far as Arianna knew, he was offering another solution to her problems, like staying in his apartment or working at the restaurant.

"Well, I'm no expert," Darius said, "but I spend enough time behind here listening to drunk people complain to know that if a lady gets a marriage proposal, she wants to know it's because the man loves her. Especially if she's already got one potential fiancé who doesn't."

In other words, Max had messed up badly. He should have told Arianna how he felt before she walked out. "I'm going to need more than one bottle," he said. It was going to take a good long drink before he stopped kicking himself. If he ever did.

Darius's hand grabbed the bottle before he could. "It's not too late, you know. You could still tell her."

"How am I supposed to do that?" Max asked, tossing back the one drink he did have. "She's halfway across the world."

The bartender arched his brow. "They've got airports, right?"

"Of course they do, but…"

"But what?"

What if going to Corinthia didn't change anything? He'd already had his heart ripped open. Was it worth getting his hopes up only to have it ripped open anew? "Who's to say she cares?"

"Who's to say she doesn't?" his friend immediately replied. "You won't know unless you ask."

Max reached for the bourbon.

"Of course, it's up to you," Darius said, grabbing the bottle before Max could and pouring out the smallest of swallows into Max's glass. "I gotta say this, though—if you'd been this cautious when we worked at Mac's, we'd still be bar-backing."

He turned and shelved the bottle with the rest of the inventory. "I better let the waitstaff know I'm closing the bar."

With that, he left Max alone to stare into his glass. Darius was right. At age eighteen, he didn't think twice about risks; he leaped at any opportunity to raise himself up. Then again, that was about making money. Failing didn't leave him feeling shattered.

Did he dare fly to Arianna and bare his soul? Was it possible she felt the same?

There was only one way to know for certain, and that was to ask her. Otherwise, he would be spending the rest of his life wondering. And if she said no...? What was the worst that could happen?

His heart didn't really have that much left to break anyway.

CHAPTER TEN

"ARE YOU SURE you're all right, sweetheart? You haven't been yourself since we left New York."

That was because she'd left part of herself behind. Noting the worry in her father's eyes, Arianna replaced the thought with a smile. "I'm fine, Father. Just a bit jet-lagged from the time change, that's all."

Her acting skills needed work because her father did not look convinced. "I wish you would tell me what is going on. You know Armando and I would do whatever we can to help."

"I know." Sadly, there was not much they could do.

After they had left Max, she'd told her father to head straight to the airport rather than stop to retrieve her luggage. The few pieces of clothing she left behind weren't worth the hardship of visiting Max's apartment. There was no way she would be able to maintain her composure while being assaulted by memories. While it had only been a few days, in her mind it felt like a lifetime. There'd been such an overwhelming sense of rightness to sharing breakfast with him, or sitting next to him on the sofa.

If her father had suspected the yearning behind her suggestion, he said nothing.

She hadn't told him about the baby yet, either. Almost did, on the plane, but she changed her mind at the last minute. In spite of everything, she felt as though Manolo deserved to hear the news first.

Hugging her midsection, she wandered from her seat on Father's sofa to the large bay window. Corinthia was readying for the holidays. The grounds crew was hanging garlands of evergreen along the palace walls. The interior had already been decorated. The tree had been erected in the archway and candles had been placed in the windows. Next door, in her mother's music room, a large spray of green sat atop the grand piano.

As they did every year, the designers had

outdone themselves. The palace was a Christmas wonderland of red, gold and purple.

It all paled in comparison to cheap store-bought garlands and a misshapen piece of plastic.

And tomorrow, when Father lit the palace tree and announced to Corinthia that the holidays had begun, it, too, would be lacking because it wasn't a snowy afternoon in Rockefeller Center, and Max wouldn't be standing behind her.

Oh, Max. She pressed her forehead against the glass. *Marry me.* His words refused to leave her alone. Every time she thought about the baby or Manolo, there they were, clear and strong. *Marry me.*

Why did he have to say anything? Why couldn't he have remained silent and simply let her go, instead of teasing her with an unachievable fantasy?

The soft knock on the door made her stomach drop. Fate had arrived. Taking a deep breath, she recovered her composure in time to see her brother's secretary, Rosa, step inside. "I'm sorry to bother you, Your Highness, but Signor Tutuola is here to see Princess Arianna."

"Manolo?" Her father's face brightened at the announcement, making her anxiety worse. "That is a surprise. How did he find out you had returned?"

"I called and asked him to come," she told him.

Her father smiled. "I would be lying if I said I wasn't pleased to hear it. I always thought the two of you made an attractive couple."

"I know." Even now, there was a smile on Father's face, eclipsing the concern that had been there the past thirty-six hours. She could but imagine how happy he would be about her and Manolo marrying.

Her father happy and her child's life scandal-free. That's why she was doing this.

"You can send him in, Rosa," she said.

When Father said they made an attractive couple, it wasn't parental bias. Manolo Tutuola was a handsome man, more runway model than industrialist. His sandy brown hair was perfectly styled, as was his closely cropped beard. When they first met, Arianna had been impressed by his sense of fashion. In a room full of men in dark suits, his flashier, continental style stood out.

That was before she'd learned what the right man could do with a simple dark suit.

Manolo flowed into the salon, and immediately bowed to her father. No extended hand for him. His protocol was flawless.

"It's good to see you again," her father said, nodding in return. "Arianna just told me she asked you to pay us a visit."

"And I was thrilled that she did. I've missed you," he said, bowing in her direction. She could see him struggling not to frown as he took in her dark hair. "You look lovely, as always."

Arianna nodded in return. She had bags under her eyes and was not wearing an ounce of makeup, not to mention that she had a foreign hair color, all of which left his sincerity open to question. "Father, would you mind if Manolo and I had a few moments alone?"

"Not at all, sweetheart. I need to speak with Armando before our meeting with the minister of finance anyway. Manolo, it is good to see you again. Perhaps we'll have the opportunity to talk afterward."

"I'd enjoy that, Your Majesty. Would you please give Signor Baldecci my best as well?

I found the interview he gave the Italian press to be quite insightful."

"I will be sure to let him know. I will see you later as well, sweetheart."

As her father leaned in to kiss her cheek, Arianna couldn't help but think it a seal of approval. "Have a good meeting, Father," she said with a smile. Manolo bowed his goodbye.

Once the door shut, he turned to look at her again, his dark eyes shining triumphantly. "I'm glad you called, Arianna. I was afraid you were going to let our misunderstanding drive a wedge between us."

"Would that be the misunderstanding where you slept with another woman?" she admonished. Crossing her arms, she marched back to her place at the window.

"I told you, Maria is just a friend who needed a place to stay. I was helping her out of a difficult situation."

"And I suppose her panties happened to appear in your bed completely by accident.

"Our laundry…"

"That's enough, Manolo." Did he really expect her to believe he was playing the Good Samaritan? A real Samaritan did not limit his good deeds to models and aspiring actresses.

He might as well learn right now that she would not be patronized. "I spoke to Maria, and I know all about your extracurricular activities. Frankly, I find your behavior, and your lies, adolescent at best."

One could call the added comment adolescent on her part as well. Considering how the man had humiliated her, however, she was owed at least one insult. The sight of his face darkening with embarrassment left a warm feeling.

It was a short-lived victory at best. Before she had a chance to say another word, he'd crossed the room to join her. "Not so childish that you didn't call and request that I visit," he replied. "Is that because you missed our... closeness as much as I did?"

She shivered as he ran an index finger along her arm. Not a good shiver, like the ones that traveled through her whenever Max came near had been, but rather a cold tremor that left a sour taste behind.

"I have missed you, Arianna," he whispered. "More than you can imagine. Just the other night I was thinking of you... How lucky I was to have you in my bed. A poor, humble servant." Lifting her hand, he brushed his lips across her knuckles.

Throughout, Arianna kept her eyes on his face and noticed that his eyes never once changed expression. There was no sign of sincerity. There wasn't even a flicker of desire. At least not on an emotional level.

No wonder instinct told her something was off about him. The man was a total phony.

"I didn't call because I missed your bed," she said, snatching her hand back. "I called because you and I needed to talk."

"All right." Taking the rejection in his stride, he leaned against the window molding. The shoulder pads of his jacket shifted, giving him a cockeyed posture. "What did you want to talk about?"

Time to bite the bullet. Arianna breathed in deeply. "I'm pregnant."

For several seconds, Manolo said nothing. "Does your father know?" he asked finally.

"Not yet. I thought..." The words tasted stale on her tongue, forcing her to swallow and start again. "I thought we could tell him together."

"Yes. That makes sense. Good thinking." He paced away, toward the center of the room. "He'll be displeased that we took so long to tell him, of course, but I can say you were afraid something was wrong, and didn't want to get his hopes up until you knew everything was going to be all right."

He glanced over his shoulder. "How far along are you anyway?"

"Nine and a half weeks."

"Great." Resuming his pacing, he began working something out in his head. "It'll be tight, but we should be able to fit in a wedding. You will definitely need to watch your diet. Plump up too much and it will show in the photographs. Although, the right designer gown should be able to camouflage any protrusion."

Camouflage? Gown? "Surely, you're not talking about having a state wedding." Considering the circumstances, would it not be better to have a small, family-only ceremony?

"Of course we're having a state wedding. We are Corinthia's most prominent couple. We can't marry with anything less than pomp and circumstance. What would people think?"

"That you wanted to keep things intimate?"

He waved her answer away with a scoff. "Are you serious? Intimate is for commoners. A royal wedding is supposed to make a statement."

Wasn't he making a statement already? Arianna's insides deflated. She perched on the windowsill, and wondered how long it would take for her to shrivel up and die. Not once had Manolo expressed any interest in the baby itself. He didn't even ask about her changed appearance. In fact, so focused was he on the logistics of their prospective union that she could have left the room without him noticing.

She didn't expect him to greet the news with hearts and flowers, but surely he could show some curiosity about his child.

"I heard the baby's heartbeat."

Manolo barely looked up at her announcement. "Good for you."

"You don't care how it went?"

He stopped his pacing to look at her. "I am sure if there was a problem, you would have told me. By the way, if we are smart, we will have the palace press office drop a few hints to the papers about an engagement. It is important that we avoid looking as though I *had* to marry you."

"Even though you did," Arianna muttered.

"Yes, but the world does not need to know that. I do business with a number of conservative countries. I do not want to give them the wrong impression."

By all means, let them protect his reputation.

Look at him, she thought, ratting off tactics like a man planning an acquisition. Wasn't he, though? Had he not won the lifetime rights to the royal family? The prize he worked so hard to attain with his charm and ingratiating behavior?

She was wrong about there being no emotion in his eyes. They gleamed with triumph.

Marry me.

She closed her eyes as Max's final plea mocked her. This was what she wanted, she reminded herself. A marriage that wouldn't haunt her with if-onlys. There would never be any doubt as to Manolo's feelings toward her. Or lack thereof. It was a cold and lonely future, but what did it matter? Without Max, her future would be cold and lonely anyway.

Suddenly, she saw herself ten years down the road, angry and alone with a child desperate for its father's attention. That was the future she was creating for her child. A life full of misery for both of them. Two unhappy people living for duty. No love. No warmth besides what they gave each other.

She thought of a woman living a joyless Christmas and a son longing to buy a tree.

Her child deserved better.

"I can't do this," she said, jumping to her feet. "I can't."

Manolo stopped his pacing and stared at her. If she didn't know better, she'd say he'd forgotten she was in the room. "What are you talking about?" he asked. "What is it that you cannot do?"

"Marry you."

"Don't be silly. You and I are having a child. We have to marry. Your father would expect no less."

"My father will have to understand." At least she prayed that he would. Either way, the die was cast. Having spoken the words, there was no way she would take them back. No way she wanted to. Free of responsibility's mantle, she felt lighter. Truer to herself. "Because there is no way I am marrying you. Not now, not ever."

"But…" When she looked back, she would probably chuckle over the stunned expression on Manolo's face. He looked as though he had been struck. This was a man who was used to succeeding. "But the baby."

"I would never keep the baby from its father. You may have as big a role in its life as you wish. Always. Just not as my husband."

"Hardly see the point otherwise."

The words were barely a whisper as he ran a hand over his face, but they were loud enough for Arianna. Her child definitely deserved better than this man. Filled with the rightness of her decision, she drew herself to full height and gave Manolo the most imperial glare she could muster. "You may go now. My secretary will keep you informed of the baby's progress."

Leaving him in the living room, she turned and disappeared into the music room.

She decided to play Chopin's *Nocturne in C minor*. The desolate-sounding concerto seemed an appropriate choice for a woman who had dismissed the father of her unborn child, was about to shame her family and was in love with a man who didn't love her back.

Mostly she played because of Max. Playing piano no longer reminded her only of her mother. Memories of playing in New York joined the mix. When her hands drifted over the keys, it was his smile of approval that she pictured. That smile was the moment when everything had begun to change. When the nerves that had been plaguing her started to shift into something more.

As for sending Manolo away, the moment she heard him mutter those words, she knew she'd done the right thing. Just as she refused Max's proposal because she didn't want to spend her days wishing he loved her, she could not marry Manolo and subject their child to the same fate. Better to live in disgrace than let her child be raised by a man who didn't love it.

Finally, she knew the answer to her no-win situation. Too bad she had to break her heart to figure it out.

Which brought her thoughts full circle back to Max. Closing her eyes, she ran through every detail of their week together. The way his voice rumbled in his chest when he stood close. How the snow dotted his hair with tiny drops of water. The warm, safe feeling she got whenever he wrapped his arms around her.

Then, after she'd remembered everything,

she folded the memories up into a tiny square and forced them into the back of her mind. From here on in, she would use what was left of her heart to be the best mother possible.

"It is good to hear music in these rooms again." At the sound of her father's voice, she opened her eyes. He stood in the doorway.

"It has been a long time since you played," he said. "Such a sad song, though, for this time of year."

Arianna switched to a carol, one of his favorites. "Better?"

"Much," he said, coming to stand behind her. She felt him press a kiss on top of her head. "It's good to have you home."

"It's good to be home," she replied, smiling. On the inside, however, she was far from cheerful, knowing this was nothing more than a brief moment of tranquility. She'd postponed the inevitable long enough.

Meanwhile, her father sat down on the settee a few feet away. It was the same piece of furniture she had sometimes napped on while her mother practiced. Out of the corner of her eye, she saw her father unbutton his jacket and settle back against the cushion.

"How was your meeting with the financial minister?" She didn't really care; it was a way of avoiding the subjects she should be discussing.

"Very well. Armando has developed a real knowledge of fiscal policy. He's going to make a very good king when I decide to step down."

"Was there ever any doubt?" Her brother took his position as heir apparent as seriously as she took her own as princess. More, actually. He would never have run off from his responsibilities. Even during the darkest days of his grief, he managed to fulfill his duties.

Had he been in her shoes, Armando no doubt would have married Manolo, too.

Her father made himself more comfortable. "I am surprised to find you alone. I assumed Manolo would be with you when I returned. Did something happen?"

Arianna's fingers slipped, and she hit a wrong note. Fortunately, Father didn't notice. "It was good to see him," he continued. "For a while, I thought the two of you might be having problems.

"Or are you still?" he asked after a pause.

It was time to stop running. Taking a deep breath, she rubbed her hands on her skirt and turned to face the one man whose opinion had always meant the world to her. "Manolo and I are no longer seeing each other," she said.

"Oh." The corners of his mouth turned downward in disappointment.

Arianna bowed her head. "I'm sorry, Father. I know you liked him."

"Very much," he replied. "I had hoped... That is, Manolo had hinted the two of you..."

"Manolo might have hoped," she said, shaking her head. "But no."

"Really? Here I thought you were fond of him."

"I tried to be." Lord knew she tried.

It was clearly not the answer her father expected, because the lines on his forehead grew more pronounced. "What do you mean 'you tried'?"

"I knew how much our being a couple meant to you. I wanted things to work out between us so that you would be happy, but in the end..."

Rising from the bench, she walked to the left-hand side of the room, where there hung a series of seventeenth-century panels by an artist whose name she never could remember. "Manolo isn't the man we thought he was." She told him about Maria and the other women. "He was more interested in currying your favor than he ever was in courting me."

"That—" Behind her, she could hear the settee cushions crinkle as her father's posture stiffened. "I treated him like a member of this family, and this is how he pays me back? By mistreating you? If I had known…"

There was another pause, and a few moments later, he was on her side of the room, drawing her into a hug. It felt disingenuous accepting the embrace, but Arianna relaxed into it anyway.

"This is why you went to New York, isn't it?" he asked. "Because of Manolo?"

"Yes…" She broke free of his arms. "And no." There was only one way to deliver the news, and that was as quickly as possible. With her hand on her stomach for strength, she looked him in the eye and said, "I'm pregnant."

You could hear a pin drop. Arianna watched as her father's expression changed from disbelief to the anger and disappointment she'd been dreading. Seeing it stabbed as deeply as she knew it would, and she ached to take it away.

"Pregnant," he finally repeated.

"I'm sorry, Father." It was the best she could do. Tears threatened to burn her eyes, but she blinked them away. Regardless of how badly his disappointment hurt, she needed to stay strong.

Somewhere in the back of her mind, a voice said Max would be proud of her for doing so.

Letting out what sounded like a low growl, he started pacing. "Manolo. He knows?"

"Yes, he does. And before you say anything, I have already told him that I would not marry him. I can't. Not knowing the kind of person he is."

She held up her hand before her father could interject. "I'm sorry. I know I've let you down, and I know it breaks with every tradition Corinthia has ever had, but please understand. I can't let my child grow up with a father who only loves himself. If I can't have a marriage like yours and Mama's, then I don't want any marriage at all. I would rather leave Corinthia than—"

"Leave Corinthia? What are you talking about?"

"To avoid a scandal. I know tradition expects me to—"

Her father stared at her in disbelief. "And you think I would ask you to leave Corinthia because of that?" he asked. "Never."

"But, the baby would be…"

"My grandchild. And you would still be my daughter. I will admit, this is not the path I expected your life to take, but I would never want you to spend your life married to a man you didn't love." Drawing close, he cradled her face in his hands. "Your happiness is far more important to me than any tradition or scandal that might erupt. Surely you know that."

Your father would want you to be happy. That was what Max had said.

She closed her eyes before the tears could break free. "I've been so stupid," she whispered.

"No, my darling daughter, I am the one who was stupid for letting you think even for a second that you had to sacrifice your happiness," her father said, gathering her in his arms.

With his arms tight around her shoulders, Arianna finally let loose the tears she'd been fighting. Outside in the courtyard, the workers were hollering about the decorations; she could hear them through the window. At the moment, though, all that mattered was that she had been afraid for nothing. She cried a little harder, this time for her foolishness.

"It's all right," her father said. He rubbed small circles on her back. "The three of us, you, me and Armando, we will deal with Manolo and any scandal he might cause. Because you are right. You should not settle for anything less than what your mother and I had."

At that, Arianna had to sniff back a fresh batch of tears. Beautiful as his words were, they made her feel more foolish. "I'm afraid it's too late for that," she said, breaking out of his embrace once more.

"Why is that?"

Suddenly, the commotion she'd heard outside grew closer. No, this was a different commotion, coming from the corridor outside the salon. "Is someone arguing with Armando?" she asked. The two of them headed into the salon, just in time to see the door fly open.

"Call the damn national guard if you want. I'm going in there," the intruder barked.

Arianna gasped.

There, in the doorway, his coat half off his shoulders, stood a wild-eyed Max Brown. "You and I need to talk," he said.

CHAPTER ELEVEN

HE'D MADE IT.

It wasn't until he'd landed in Corinthia and saw the large royal portrait hanging in the airport that Max discovered a major flaw in his plan. This wasn't New York, where all he had to do was unlock his penthouse door to see Arianna. Visiting her here was going to be like trying to see the President of the United States. A person couldn't walk into the palace and ask for Arianna Santoro. You needed a royal invitation or special permission, which could take days—or weeks—to wrangle.

He didn't have days to spare. Not with Arianna planning to marry Manolo and leave his life forever.

Fortunately for him, he still had Vittorio Mastella's business card in his pocket. Either the head of security had a romantic streak, or he appreciated Max's skills as a fast talker, because he agreed to let Max pass through security without credentials.

"You are on your own after that," he'd said. "If Her Highness refuses to see you, I will throw you out personally."

Max had no intention of that happening. Not even when Arianna's brother tried to bar him access, and he had to push his way through.

Now, he was face-to-face with Arianna at last.

She looked horrible, eyes puffy and red-rimmed, her skin the color of chalk. "You and I need to talk," he said. With all the adrenaline of the last few minutes, the words came out far harsher than he meant, so he added in a gentler voice, "Please."

He'd just finished shrugging his jacket into place when a hand clamped down on his upper arm. "I'm sorry, Father. He pushed his way through," its owner said. "Security is on the way."

"It's all right, Armando. I know him." Arianna's eyes were two large pools of blue, shimmering with surprise and...were those tears?

His stomach clenched. The pallor, the

crying… Wrenching himself free, he rushed closer only to stop short of taking her in his arms. He wanted to—God knew, holding her again was all he thought about since leaving New York—but the despair in her eyes held him back. "Are you okay?" he asked. "Is the baby…?"

"The baby is fine," she replied. Max let out his breath. He hadn't realized how scared he'd been to hear her answer until she alleviated his concerns. If there had been any doubt in his mind about raising another man's child, it died then and there. Who cared who fathered the child? The baby was part of Arianna; therefore he loved it with all of his heart.

Loved it with all of his heart. Who would have guessed those words would ever enter his thoughts? He, who avoided love like the plague.

"What are you doing here?" Arianna asked.

"I told you. I needed to talk to you."

She hadn't moved since he burst into the room. Now, she walked toward one of the room's large windows, her hands twisting back and forth in front of her.

"What could we possibly have to talk about that we did not say in New York?" she asked.

A lot. Their entire lives. "Just give me five minutes. After that, if you want me to go, I'll leave and never bother you again."

Blood pounded in his ears thanks to his racing heart. *Please let her say yes.*

She didn't answer.

"I think you should leave now, Signor Brown." It was King Carlos. Focused on Arianna as he was, he'd forgotten the king was in the room. "My daughter obviously does not wish to see you."

Turning slowly, he looked at the man Arianna served so devotedly. "If you don't mind, I'd rather hear that from her directly."

"Who do you think you are? Do you have any idea who you are talking to?"

Arianna's brother—at least he assumed it was Arianna's brother—reached for his arm again, only this time Max was ready and sidestepped the attempt. He backed toward the window as well, meeting the gazes of the king and his son glare for glare. They could try and intimidate him all they wanted. He wasn't leaving unless Arianna threw him out herself.

From the corner of his eye, he saw Arianna hang her head. "Let him stay," she said in a soft voice. "I'll listen to what he has to say."

"Alone," he added. Again, King Carlos and his son glared at him. Again, he returned the glares.

"It's okay," Arianna added. "I'm not in any danger."

Far from it, Max wanted to say. If anyone was in danger it was him. One well-placed rejection, and his heart would shatter.

"That might be the first time anyone has ever ordered them to do anything," she said once the others left the room.

"Thank you for backing me up."

"The only reason I did was to avoid a scene." Finally she turned away from the window to look at him. "Why are you here?"

Max opened, and then shut his mouth. He'd had an entire speech planned, but seeing her up close, the late-day light behind her forming a gray silhouette, all his impressive words failed him. The only thing he could come up with was "You left your suitcase."

"I decided I didn't need it. Is that why you flew halfway around the world? To return my luggage?"

"No."

"I didn't think so." She looked down as if just noticing her twitching hands and quickly clasped them tight. "So what did you want?"

Was there a note of expectation in her question? His quickening pulse said yes, but he refused to get his hopes up. "Are you still planning to marry Manolo?"

She answered with a haughty sniff before walking away. "I don't think that's any of your business."

None of his business, but she hadn't said yes.

He followed her into the next room, which turned out to be a lavishly decorated space containing a very large piano. Arianna was making a production out of straightening a pile of sheet music, a portrait of anger and sadness. He wondered what she would do if he rested his hands on her shoulders and cradled her close. "Why did you turn my proposal down?" he asked instead. "Why did you walk away?"

"Because…"

"'Because' isn't an answer." Why was he dragging this out? The words *I love you* were right on his tongue. All he needed to do was say them.

But he was still afraid. He needed to know this wasn't one-sided. "Was it because you didn't think I meant it?"

"No. I know you meant it."

"Then…?"

"Because I didn't want to be another one of your charity cases, that's why!" Music scattered to the carpet as she whipped around. "I didn't want to be someone you had to rescue. I wanted…"

"Wanted what?" Max asked, heart pounding.

She looked away again. "Nothing."

There was no need for her to answer; he knew. He heard it in the way her voice cracked when she spoke. And with that confession, the last of fear's grip on his heart disappeared.

Slowly, he reached out to brush the hair from her cheek. "You were never a charity case," he told her. "Not for a second."

"Of course I was. I was no different than Darius or Shirley or any of the others who crossed your path," she said. But she leaned into his touch nonetheless, giving him the confidence to carry on.

"Do you remember the first time we shared

a taxi? You said people do crazy things when they're in love. Remember?"

"I remember."

Her breath hitched. Closing his eyes, Max pressed a kiss to her temple. Being close to her again was like coming home after a long absence. "Does flying halfway around the world to stop a wedding count as crazy?" he whispered in her hair.

Arianna's heart stopped. Was he saying what she thought he was saying? She was afraid to look him in the face, in case this was all a sick, terrible joke.

But here he was, holding her. His fingers tracing her jaw. Lifting her chin until she had no choice but to look into his eyes.

Which stared down at her with slate-blue sincerity. "I'm not rescuing you," he whispered, his words hoarse with emotion. "You're the one rescuing me. I need you in my life."

Was he saying…?

"I love you, Arianna."

They were the most beautiful four words she'd ever heard. Words she had hoped and wished for, but never thought she'd hear pass his lips. "I love you, too," she whispered, and she kissed him with all the love she had in her heart. A deep, soul-searing kiss meant to say everything she couldn't put into words.

It ended much too soon. She could have stayed that way forever, wrapped in his arms, but suddenly Max backed away, his eyes bright and unreadable.

"I'm not finished," he said with a smile.

With that, he dropped to his knee. "Marry me, Arianna. Tell Manolo and your father and everyone else to go to blazes and marry me. I promise I will spend the rest of our lives making you and the baby happy."

He already had. She was happier at this moment than she could ever remember. So happy, she couldn't hold back the tears. "Yes," she said, dropping to her knees and throwing her arms around his neck. "Yes, yes, yes."

They clung to each other, laughing and crying at the same time. "I love you," Max repeated over and over. "I love you."

When they'd recovered, he brushed back the hair from her face. "I never thought to bring a ring."

Arianna laughed. Later, she would tell him about dismissing Manolo and her talk with her father. What mattered now was that they were going to spend the rest of their life together. "It doesn't matter," she whispered against his lips. "I have you."

EPILOGUE

MAX LIFTED TWO glasses of sparkling cider from the tray on the table, and handed one to his bride. "So what time does Babbo Natale show up?"

"I don't know. I told you, Armando and I always fell asleep before his arrival."

"In other words, this whole thing is an excuse to stay up all night."

"Would you rather we fall asleep early?"

"Absolutely not. I can't think of a better way to spend Christmas Eve than under a tree with you." He clinked the rim of his glass against hers. "Merry Christmas, Your Highness."

"That's Mrs. Brown to you," Arianna replied. She giggled as the carbonation danced over her tongue.

Officially, they were now to be referred to as Conte di Corinthia, Prince Maxwell, and

Her Royal Highness Princess Arianna, but she liked plain old Mr. and Mrs. Max Brown. The names had a simple, sincere ring to them.

The two of them were sequestered in their new private quarters at the palace, having been married exactly twelve hours. Tomorrow, Christmas Day, they would be officially presented to Corinthia as husband and wife. Tonight, however, was about them. Knowing the pomp and circumstance that awaited them, Arianna wanted their wedding night to last as long as possible. Apparently Max agreed because when she came up with the idea of staying awake for Babbo Natale, he enthusiastically agreed.

She curled closer to her husband, draping the sheer robe of her peignoir across their laps like a blanket. Nearby, next to the fireplace, a tree laden with white lights twinkled merrily. "I might be biased," she said, "but as beautiful as that tree is, it is nothing compared to the one at the Fox Club. That might be the most beautiful tree I've ever seen."

"Better than the one in Rockefeller Center?"

"Absolutely. You didn't kiss me behind the one at Rockefeller Center."

"Ah, good point, Mrs. Brown." He bent his head over hers. "I can, however, kiss you under this one."

"Mmm, as much as you want," she replied. There would be a lifetime of kisses under Christmas trees. Not to mention children laughing and begging for their own late night Christmas Eves. This was but the first night of forever.

As she'd suspected, Manolo was far more interested in making royal connections than he was in being a father. Therefore, it wasn't a surprise when he agreed to let Max adopt the child as his own. It also wasn't a surprise that Max refused to let Father make Manolo sign away his parental rights. "Someday he might realize what an idiot he is," he'd said.

Perhaps, but Arianna suspected that would never happen. She and Max would raise the child—their child—in a home filled with family and love.

With a happy sigh, she thought of the smile on her father's face as they said their vows. Who would have guessed that in risking his disappointment, she'd made him happier than ever? "Thank you for agreeing to have the wedding in Corinthia."

"I've already told you, I didn't care where we got married, so long as we did. Besides," he said, nuzzling her neck, "watching Darius having to bow to your father and brother was totally worth it."

"That was your favorite part of the ceremony?"

"Second favorite," he said. "Hearing you say 'I do' was the best part."

Arianna had to admit, that was her favorite part, too.

Her eyes were getting heavy. Apparently when it came to dragging out her wedding night, the spirit was willing, but the pregnant body was not. She nuzzled closer to Max, letting his scent lull her to sleep.

Suddenly, a rippling sensation traveled across her abdomen. Like bubbles. Instantly, she awoke and grabbed Max's hand.

"What—?"

"Shh…" she said, placing his hand on her stomach. "Feel that?"

The ripple repeated.

His jaw dropped. "Is that…?"

"I think the baby is trying to wish us a merry Christmas."

Nothing in the world would ever match the

smile that split Max's face. She wanted to weep with happiness at the joy that shone in his eyes. "Not *the* baby," he said. "*Our* baby."

Leaning over, he placed a kiss right above her belly button before returning to kiss her. "Merry Christmas, Princess."

As far as she was concerned, it already was.

* * * *

For more Corinthian Christmas magic, don't miss Prince Armando's story in WINTER WEDDING FOR THE PRINCE.

To learn more about WINTER WEDDING FOR THE PRINCE as well as Barbara Wallace's other titles, visit www.barbarawallace.com.

COMING NEXT MONTH FROM

ⓗ HARLEQUIN®

Romance

Available December 6, 2016

#4547 WINTER WEDDING FOR THE PRINCE
Royal House of Corinthia • by Barbara Wallace

Crown Prince Armando enlists royal assistant Rosa Lamberti to help him find a suitable wife, but a surprise kiss under the mistletoe awakens feelings he thought long buried! Rosa is shocked to realize she yearns to be Armando's bride... Will she get the best Christmas gift of all—her own royal wedding?

#4548 CHRISTMAS IN THE BOSS'S CASTLE
Maids Under the Mistletoe • by Scarlet Wilson

Chambermaid Grace Ellis loves Christmas, but she's spending this season working. So when her boss, Finlay "Scrooge" Armstrong, offers her a magical Christmas in Scotland, she can't resist! Snowbound in his castle, Grace starts to melt the ice around widower Finlay's heart. He never thought he'd love again, but could Grace be his Christmas miracle?

#4549 HER FESTIVE DOORSTEP BABY
by Kate Hardy

When baby Hope is left on Amy Howes's doorstep on Christmas Eve, enigmatic but gorgeous neighbor Dr. Josh Farnham is there to lend her a helping hand. Although they both have demons to fight, Josh and Amy forge a bond as unexpected as it is heart-stopping. This little Hope could change their lives forever!

#4550 HOLIDAY WITH THE MYSTERY ITALIAN
by Ellie Darkins

When paralyzed tycoon Mauro Evans stars in a charity dating show, he can't resist the challenge of picking prickly Amber Harris to take on holiday! Amber's determined to ignore his attraction, but Mauro's bravery threatens to tear down her defenses and give her a new Christmas dream—ringing in the New Year with wedding bells!

YOU CAN FIND MORE INFORMATION ON UPCOMING HARLEQUIN® TITLES, FREE EXCERPTS AND MORE AT WWW.HARLEQUIN.COM.

"Have you ever looked at an unfocused telescope only to turn the knob and make everything sharp and clear?" Armando asked.

Rosa nodded.

"That is what it was like for me a few minutes ago. One moment I had all these sensations I couldn't explain swirling inside me, then the next everything made sense. It was my soul coming back to life."

"I don't know what to think," she said.

"Then don't think," he replied. "Just go with your heart."

He made it sound easy. *Just go with your heart.* But what if your heart was frightened and confused? For all his talk of coming to life, he was essentially in the same place as before, unable or unwilling to give her a true emotional commitment.

On the other hand, her feelings wanted to override her common sense, so maybe they were even. As she watched him close the gap between them, she felt her heartbeat quicken to match her breath.

"You do know that we're under the mistletoe yet again, don't you?"

The sprig of berries had quite a knack for timing, didn't it? Anticipation ran down her spine, ceasing what little hold common sense still had. Armando was going to kiss her and she was going to let him. She wanted to lose herself in his arms. Believe for a moment that his heart felt more than simple desire for her.

This time, when he wrapped his arm around her waist, she slid against him willingly, aligning her hips against his with a smile.

"Appears to be our fate," she whispered. "Mistletoe, that is."

"You'll get no complaints from me." She could hear her heart beating in her ears as his head dipped toward hers. "Merry Christmas, Rosa."

"Mer..." His kiss swallowed the rest of her wish. Rosa didn't care if she spoke another word again. She'd waited her whole life to be kissed like this. Fully and deeply, with a need she felt all the way down to her toes.

They were both breathless when the moment ended. With their foreheads resting against each other, she felt Armando smile against her lips. "Merry Christmas," he whispered again.

Don't miss
WINTER WEDDING FOR THE PRINCE
by Barbara Wallace,
available December 2016 wherever
Harlequin® Romance books and ebooks are sold.

www.Harlequin.com

HREXP1116

Reading Has Its Rewards

Earn **FREE BOOKS!**

Register at **Harlequin My Rewards** and submit your Harlequin purchases from wherever you shop to earn points for free books and other exclusive rewards.

Plus submit your purchases from now till May 30th for a chance to win a $500 Visa Card*.

Visit **HarlequinMyRewards.com** today

MYR16R1